"You are staying right where you are until you climb the stairs and sleep in my bed."

Her belly dropped, a delicious sensation both full and fluttery. Hearing his low voice commanding her to sleep in his bed ticked several boxes in the attributes of her fantasy guy. Which made no sense. She didn't like Max. Not like that.

"I, uh, I need to get to the hotel, Max." Especially since she felt that same attraction to him she had when she'd first knocked on his front door. This was beyond inconvenient.

"Chains or no, this weather's no good for driving. I'm not risking us being caught out in this again. You need to rest and stay warm. Do you want tea?"

His gruff voice was firm and unyielding, yet beyond the gravel, she heard something else. Care. Max cared about her enough to keep her safe and warm.

* * *

Million-Dollar Mix-Up by Jessica Lemmon
is part of The Dunn Brothers series.

Dear Reader,

Max and Isaac Dunn are twin brothers who have a history on television. They grew up portraying the same character on a wildly popular hit show a few decades ago. Think Mary-Kate and Ashley Olsen on *Full House* but with guys. ;)

Two decades later, Isaac is holed up on his private island preparing for the reprisal of his childhood role, which he's taking on solo this time around. Meanwhile, Isaac's agent, Kendall Squire, has promised a prominent company he'd film a commercial for them, and she needs him in LA in two days. What's a talent agent with one remaining client to do? Hunt down Isaac's identical twin and beg Max to take his brother's place, that's what. There's just one teensy-weensy problem. Max has sworn off acting— *permanently*.

Now that Kendall is trapped in a snowbound cabin with the grumpy former actor, she's beginning to wish she'd never stepped foot on Million Dollar Mountain. But after a searing hot tub kiss, she learns that Max is more than a surly mountain man with a chip on his shoulder. And he's offering her way more than she'd bargained for when she planned a "quick" trip to the East Coast...

I hope you enjoy Max and Kendall's story as much as I enjoyed writing it. Make room on your keeper shelf, because Isaac and Meghan's book is coming up next.

Happy reading!

Jessica Lemmon

Sign up for my newsletter: www.jessicalemmon.com.
Become a member: www.lemmonadestand.com.

JESSICA LEMMON

MILLION-DOLLAR MIX-UP

HARLEQUIN®
DESIRE™

Recycling programs
for this product may
not exist in your area.

ISBN-13: 978-1-335-73544-7

Million-Dollar Mix-Up

Copyright © 2022 by Jessica Lemmon

This edition published by arrangement with Harlequin Books S.A.

For questions and comments about the quality of this book,
please contact us at CustomerService@Harlequin.com.

Harlequin Enterprises ULC
22 Adelaide St. West, 41st Floor
Toronto, Ontario M5H 4E3, Canada
www.Harlequin.com

Printed in U.S.A.

A former job-hopper, **Jessica Lemmon** resides in Ohio with her husband and rescue dog. She holds a degree in graphic design, which is currently gathering dust in an impressive frame. When she's not writing supersexy heroes, she can be found cooking, drawing, drinking coffee (okay, wine) and eating potato chips. She firmly believes God gifts us with talents for a purpose, and with His help, you can create the life you want.

Jessica is a social media junkie who loves to hear from readers. You can learn more at jessicalemmon.com.

Books by Jessica Lemmon

Harlequin Desire

Kiss and Tell

His Forbidden Kiss
One Wild Kiss
One Last Kiss

Dynasties: Beaumont Bay

Second Chance Love Song
Good Twin Gone Country

The Dunn Brothers

Million-Dollar Mix-Up

Visit her Author Profile page at Harlequin.com, or jessicalemmon.com, for more titles.

You can also find Jessica Lemmon on Facebook, along with other Harlequin Desire authors, at Facebook.com/harlequindesireauthors!

One

Kendall Squire was not dressed for the weather.

As she maneuvered carefully up snowy Million Dollar Mountain—who named these things, any-way?—she took one hand off the steering wheel to adjust the vent so heat would blow on her frigid toes. High-heeled, open-toed booties were perfect for Los Angeles. Snowy Virginia mountains on the other hand? Not so much.

She ran the script in her mind once again about what she'd say when she encountered the man she was driving here to see. He didn't know she was com-ing, and after much debate back in sunny California, Kendall opted not to warn him of her arrival. Not because she wanted to ambush him, but because she wasn't sure he wouldn't tell her no over the phone. She was more persuasive in person, anyway.

At least, she usually was. She'd been working sixteen-hour days at the talent agency since her mentor Lou, the owner and head agent of Legacy, up and retired. No one had seen it coming since he was barely fifty years old. He sold the company and waved goodbye to her and the rest of their team, but not before bequeathing his elite client list.

Her divvied portion was impressive. *Was* being the operative word. When she'd contacted her new clients to introduce herself, she was met with a variety of responses. Unfriendly at worst, apologetic at best. One by one they fired her—as per their contracts any handing over from Lou to another agent was a loophole that allowed them to leave. It seemed no one trusted a "baby agent" to oversee their illustrious careers. She was thirty-four years old, hardly a baby, but she'd kept the argument to herself.

Her last phone call, made with shaking hands and a tremor of fear in her belly, had been to Isaac Dunn. Isaac was one half of the twin brother duo who had played Danny Brooks on the wildly popular *Brooks Knows Best* sitcom, airing twenty years ago. From ages five through fifteen, Isaac and his twin brother, Max, grew up on screen portraying the son of Samuel and Pauline Brooks, who lived with their extended family, a league of warm, fun, trouble-causing cousins. The show had recently been resuscitated on a streaming service, with an anniversary miniseries to air in a year's time. Fans of the show were already abuzz, gossiping about plot scenarios and returning love interests for Danny. No longer a fan of the silver screen, Max had retired from acting decades ago, leaving Isaac to reprise the role solo. Max's answer to returning to the show had been a clear *no*. Kendall had feared a similar response from Isaac about accepting her as his new representation.

But the phone call had gone better than she'd expected. She'd called and introduced herself, and had learned that Lou called Isaac personally to let him know of the change-up. In turn, she promised to be the best agent Isaac ever had, and swore not to let him down. The trip she was making to visit his twin brother on this mountaintop had everything to do with her keeping that promise. She wouldn't let her only remaining client down.

Kendall's phone rang from her purse, pulling her from her ruminations. Her rental car answered on speaker, allowing her to keep both hands on the steering wheel as she navigated the slick terrain. The screen on the dashboard read *Meghan Squire*. Her younger sister.

"Hey, Meg."

"Hiiiii!" Meghan practically sang. Kendall's sister was a bright burst of joy on most days, but today her voice was extra chirpy. "Are you there yet?"

"You sound breathless. Are you feeling all right?" Kendall asked through a big smile.

"Don't leave me in suspense! I'm dying!"

"I'm not there yet. I'm driving through acres of

snow-covered mountains at the moment. Who knew it was this cold in Virginia?"

"Well, hurry up and get there and then videophone me in secret so I can spy on the reclusive, mysterious Max Dunn. Do you think you can convince him to do an exclusive interview with me? Please, please, *pleeeease*?"

Meghan hosted, and had founded, a wildly popular podcast called *Superfan TV*. The topic of every episode was television sitcoms in the past, ranging from murder mysteries to court shows to light, frothy family dramadies. *Brooks Knows Best* happened to be at the top of Meghan's favorites list.

"I promise if the opportunity to mention it comes up, I'll ask," Kendall told her sister. "I'm not sure Max is going to be amenable to his brother's agent begging for his help on a commercial, let alone my pimping a podcast interview about a show he's not going to be on."

"I know."

Kendall practically heard her sister deflate.

"Isaac might do it, though," she couldn't help offering. She had no idea if that was true, especially since Isaac wasn't in the continental US, but from what she'd read online, and knew of the two brothers personally, Isaac was more laid-back than Max.

"Really?" Meghan's voice was imbued with hope.

"Give me a week or so. I have to convince Max to help me out, fly back to LA, do a commercial shoot, and then lure Isaac back to California. I have a busy month ahead."

"You lead a glamorous life, sis. Here I sit in a rented farmhouse alone, watching the barn cat chase something in the high grass."

"Don't rub it in. You know I'm dealing with ice and snow."

Meghan laughed, then seemed to sober. "There was one more reason for my call."

Kendall had suspected as much.

"I wanted to check on you. Are you okay?"

"Of course," came Kendall's automatic answer. But she knew Meghan was asking out of more than curiosity.

"It's his birthday today," her sister said quietly.

"I know." Kendall pulled a deep breath in through her nose, the white landscape in front of her blurring as she pictured her older brother's big, toothy smile and midlength curly blond hair. He was twenty when he died. She'd never forgiven him for leaving their family so abruptly. She needed him. Then. And now. "And yes, I'm okay. How are you?"

"I'm good. I like to remember him on this day, you know. Send up a little prayer to check on him, and then go back to doing what I love. You should do the same."

It was easier for Meghan, she supposed. Kendall had been sixteen when Quinton died. Meghan had been eleven. Not that Meg had loved him any less, but Quin had been closest with Kendall. His leaving had left a huge mark on her soul that'd never fully healed.

"That's good advice." Kendall forced a smile. She

talked to Quin sometimes, too, but her prayers were packed with questions like, *Why did you have to go on the trip that summer? Why couldn't you have stayed home with me?*

"Tell Max your adoring sister and *Brooks Knows Best*'s biggest fan says hello. Be safe and call me ASAP!"

"Will do." Kendall told Meghan she loved her— an opportunity they'd rarely missed since their brother had passed—and ended the call.

Right on time, too. Her tires skidded in the gathering snow as a cabin came into view. Her GPS had put her at .01 miles from her destination about two miles ago. Since this town wasn't well documented on satellite imaging, she hadn't been sure when, or if, she'd encounter a residence.

This one was hard to miss. The massive log cabin was at least two stories, three if you counted what looked like an attic space with three dormers, and sitting off the road. The cabin was surrounded by a rustic fence that looked more stylized than like actual worn boards. As she maneuvered closer, she noted the modern iron lighting fixtures and overall pristine cleanliness of the property and decided this was definitely Max's place.

He'd left LA with plenty of money and relocated to Virginia, but he hadn't moved to this town until ten years later. Shortly after, the town changed its name to its current one: Dunn, coined after the man who'd bought up most of it. There was reclusive, and then there was Max Dunn. According to online rumors, he had absconded to the mountains of Virginia to hide out and purchased a town to do it in.

She parked off to the side next to a large, three-car garage, also log-cabin style to match the mansion. The numbers on the structure confirmed she was at the right place. 102 Brooks Boulevard. She wondered if the town had named the street after the show Max had starred in, or if it was a wild coincidence. *Fate*, her sister might call it.

Kendall wasn't as susceptible to believing life had a plan. It seemed random, tossing its inhabitants into the wind and delighting when they fell to the ground disoriented.

She climbed out of her toasty car, left her purse behind and pocketed her cell phone. She tromped through the gathering snow, yipping when some of the cold white stuff settled into her open-toed booties. Definitely the wrong shoes for this excursion. But they were her lucky shoes. She'd purchased them with money from her first real pay bump at the agency.

Steeling herself for laying eyes on Isaac's identical twin for the first time, she straightened her back and knocked on the door.

And waited.

After what seemed like a very long time of jumping up and down to keep warm, she heard shuffling coming from inside. She pictured him unkempt, maybe with a scraggly mass of overgrown hair, pot belly, perhaps wearing a stained T-shirt. Then the door swung aside and blew her vision to smithereens.

Max filled the threshold with his hulking, dark presence. His hair was a bit long, but he was well-groomed, from the top of his head to a thick, dark beard. He was fit and trim, a waffle-pattern dark blue Henley stretched over his flat belly. The rest of his outfit was standard Paul Bunyan attire: a flannel and jeans, and he wore both very, very well.

Kendall's smile fell, her eyes roaming over him before once again landing on his face. Then they froze there, much like she was freezing on his covered patio, but the sensation of being under his stare was infinitely more pleasant.

She blinked at the rugged replica of Isaac Dunn, momentarily at a loss for words. Max was, after all, Isaac's *identical* twin so she'd expected them to look alike. What she hadn't expected was a blast of attraction hitting her like air from a hot oven. Especially when it was this freaking cold outside.

While Isaac was without a doubt an attractive guy, so were a lot of the guys in Hollywood. Seeing an attractive male specimen wasn't a rarity in LA. She could throw a rock and hit a smirking, godlike male, ranging from golden to bronze in color, and representing every precious metal in between.

She'd objectively appreciated the attractiveness of Isaac's strong nose, his height and his smile, but Max emitted grade-A pheromones like smoke from a roaring fire.

He stood in his doorway, his brow crinkled, his lips frowning behind that perfectly groomed beard. He appeared dark and dangerous, and since her libido had been neglected for the past six months, damn sexy.

She must've been more tired than she'd originally thought if she was staring mute at the brother of her client. Snapping out of her shock, which wasn't hard to do when a gust of frigid wind spiraled through the open porch and wrapped around her legs, she forced a confident smile.

"Max Dunn?" she asked, even though there was no reason to ask. He was clearly Isaac's twin. "H-hi," she continued clumsily. "Kendall. Squire. I'm Isaac's agent. Talent agent."

Pull it together.

Max's blue eyes grew darker, his frown deepening. Now he looked like a rugged, *angry* mountain man, but no less sexy.

He sent a brief gaze down her leather coat to her boots and back up to where snow was melting in her hair. "Everything all right?"

Whether it was the sincerity reflecting in his ocean-blue eyes or fatigue from her long journey here, she wasn't sure, but she replied to his question with honesty.

"I've had a tough couple of months. Years, actually." Her gaze flitted to a pile of split logs stacked against the side of the house. "But I've always been a firm believer in moving forward. One step after the last, you know?"

His frown carved a dent between his eyebrows, then those fantastic, thick brows lifted and he simply stared at her, his expression blank. "I'm sorry to hear of your troubles, but I was asking if everything was all right with Isaac. Assuming that's why you're here."

Heat infused her cheeks as she retraced the conversation. "Oh. Of course. I knew that." She swallowed thickly, not easy to do with her teeth chattering. "Yes, he's fine. Great, actually. Well, not great. I mean *he's* great, but his career could use a, uh… There's something going on in LA and we need him, but he's on an island. That he owns. I had no idea he owned an island." She couldn't seem to stop rambling. "Anyway, he's stuck there."

"Stuck?" Max's eyebrows lifted.

"On purpose," she added. "The pilot is on vacation, which Isaac knew. So, he's there in a cabana. Or a mansion. I don't actually know what kind of housing." She frowned to herself, realizing she didn't know much about her client at all. Best get to the point. "I need him in LA in two days and he can't make it, I guess is what I'm trying to say. Which is why I stopped by to see you. I was hoping we could talk. Do you have a minute?"

Two

The last time a beautiful woman was in his presence asking him if he had a minute was... Well, it was about an hour ago.

But this wasn't his irritating ex-wife, Bunny, clomping around on his custom wood flooring in her fur-lined boots. This woman wasn't wearing boots. Or, rather, she was, but they were the most impractical boots he'd ever seen. He grimaced at the open-toed, high-heeled, poor excuses for footwear. She'd clearly blown in from the West Coast. From her hair, dark-with-caramel-blond-highlights, to her sun-kissed, golden, flawless skin, to the rest of her wardrobe: designer jeans and a leather coat meant more for style than warmth, she didn't belong here.

And as she'd just stated—in a roundabout way—

Isaac was needed for something in LA and was "stuck" on his private island, so she'd come to Max. He assumed Ms. Squire was here to ask him to step in and take Isaac's place. He'd been asked to pretend to be his brother during his entire life growing up—mostly for the television show they'd starred in, but also off the clock. He'd stepped in to be Isaac whenever Isaac hadn't been able to be in two places at once, and his brother had done the same for Max on occasion.

He was about to open his mouth and tell her thanks but no thanks, but he reconsidered. She was standing on his front porch, her arms braced over her chest and shivering. Hell, he couldn't turn her away now. No matter she was from his least favorite place on the planet. He walked away from fantasyland when he was twenty years old, vowing never to return to LA or to his former profession, but he had no grudge against this woman. Snow fell faster behind her, gathering on her car parked in front of his garage. Before he sent her on her way, he'd allow her to warm up.

"Come on in, California."

The nickname took her by surprise, her eyes rounding briefly. Then she smiled at him, bouncing a little on her toes, which he imagined were frozen solid by now. "Really? Thank you."

He left the door open and allowed her to come inside his not-so-humble abode. His cabin had space and privacy, two things he treasured most in this world. There were windows along the back, doors opening to a balcony overlooking hills and mountains alike. To either side were acres of woods. His home was shrouded with trees, tucked back into the woodland like it was part of the scenery. He loved it here.

He let her walk in ahead of him, catching a whiff of clean cotton and sunshine, like she'd brought a bit of the West Coast with her to Virginia.

Inside, he closed the door, and walked to the kitchen. He flipped on a gas burner and set a kettle over the flame, turning his head to notice Kendall slipping out of her high-heeled boots to shuffle across his floors barefoot. Quite different from Bunny's stomping and tromping while she complained to him once again that he wasn't helping her "achieve my dreams, Max." He'd heard similar complaints a time or twelve during their marriage, and had hoped a divorce would be the end of talk of his ties with the acting world. Not so. Bunny had shown up like a bad penny asking again if he could call his brother and land her a walk-on role on the *Brooks Knows Best* reprisal.

"Nice place." Kendall padded over to the living room. She was taller than Bunny, too, not that he had any reason to notice. Kendall stood in front of the fireplace stocked with split wood and newspaper. He'd been about to light it before she knocked. "You and your brother live very different lives."

"Not really. We both like being alone." Not true of Isaac. He didn't know why he'd said that. Maybe because talk of Isaac made him tense. Max was the oldest by a mere seventy-two seconds. Other than their identical physical features, he couldn't be more different from his twin. Max had walked away from fame gladly. Isaac had stayed—and by proxy forced Max into staying—for years after *Brooks Knows Best* aired its last episode. By age twenty, Max let his brother and his agent know he was done with the promotional crap that rode shotgun with fame. No more meet-and-greets. *Period.* Isaac had argued no one wanted to meet "just one Dunn." And if Max refused to show, the invitations for Isaac would dry up, as well.

The feud between them hadn't lasted forever— but five years had felt close to it. By the time they'd both agreed to show up at their parents' house one Christmas, the damage was done. Sure, they were cordial, and had chatted over bourbons by the fireplace, but they weren't as close as they once were. Max figured they never would be.

He held no real animosity toward his brother. They were simply two different people with their eyes on two different prizes. One of them wanted to be out of the spotlight, the other bathed in it.

"Well, at least you're not stranded." Kendall had a pretty smile. It shook at the edges, either from the chill she'd caught outside in those impractical boots, or maybe nerves. She didn't seem shy, but he was definitely picking up on some sort of tension.

"Not yet." He'd break the bad news that she could be stranded if she stayed too long, but he'd wait until after she warmed up. She might not make it down the mountain at this point anyway. "Have a seat."

He filled two mugs with hot water, dropping a tea bag into his and offering her a selection.

"Thank you." Her gratitude was evident, which struck him as funny. Who was infinitely grateful over tea? "Oh, licorice."

"Good choice."

She sat down at his table, a big, broad wooden slab surrounded by handmade chairs, and tucked one foot under her thigh. She'd kept her coat on and he figured it was just as well. She needed to warm up, but she also needed to leave soon. At the rate the snow fell outside, if she stayed much longer, she wouldn't make it out of his driveway.

"The reason I'm here, Mr. Dunn—"

"Max."

She smiled prettily again, her chocolate-brown eyes warming a few degrees. "Max. The reason I'm here is because I have an opportunity for you. I think you'll find quite intriguing."

He nearly chuckled. An opportunity to her sounded like an inconvenience to him. But he let her go on.

"As you know, your brother is returning to *Brooks Knows Best* and preparing to reprise the role of Danny alone." Her brows bent in sympathy, like she couldn't puzzle out why Max had turned down the opportunity to pop in and play a minor role on the show. The fans would have loved it, but he was living his life his way this time around. He didn't merely do things to make money or to please fans. Not anymore.

"Anyway, Isaac has a lucrative offer to film a commercial with Citizen watches. Unfortunately, he, ah, well, he can't make it back in time to film the commercial. It'll take a few hours, tops. There are no lines to remember. It's scheduled to be filmed on a closed set in two days. All you would have to do is show up and do the shoot. Then you can fly back to this beautiful, snowy wonderland and pretend it never happened." She gestured outside and then clasped her hands together, her smile broad, her tone hinting she fully expected a yes.

Damn. He knew answering his door was going to be inconvenient. Moreover, part of him didn't want to tell this beautiful woman no. She'd come a long way and was clearly excited about her brilliant plan. But he had to tell her no. For myriad reasons, not the least of which was—

"You're asking me to pretend to be Isaac."

"I'm asking you to be in a commercial where the Citizen watch folks will *assume* you're Isaac." She avoided his eyes, focusing instead on dunking the tea bag into her mug of water. "Pretending, that's what acting is, right?"

It was so much more than pretending, but he'd queue that speech for another day. He was already spent from arguing with Bunny. He didn't have energy reserved for Kendall.

"I'm out of the acting business. And there is zero

chance of me *pretending* to be Isaac in a commercial. Sorry. You've wasted your time."

"Citizen sent me half a dozen watches for promo," she continued as if he hadn't spoken. "Men's and women's styles. I brought them with me. You're welcome to any or all of them. If you're not familiar, the brand is high-end and very luxurious."

"Look around, California. What the hell do I need a watch for?"

She did look around, turning her head left and right and then looking over her shoulder at the stairs leading to the second floor. A tiny unicorn pendant on a gold chain dipped into the hollow of her throat when she took a deep breath. Then those brown eyes were on his again and her smile set to *stun*.

"Do it for Isaac, then. He's on the cusp of making a huge comeback. The press is salivating for details about the show's reunion. I know you've turned down offers for a walk-on role and interviews, but this is your chance to contribute while keeping your distance. You can help him without thrusting yourself into the limelight."

"I helped my brother navigate those piranha-infested waters for fifteen years, Ms. Squire. That's enough to last two lifetimes. My answer is no."

Her smile shook at the edges before she busied herself with sipping her tea and commenting that it was "very good." She blew out a breath he thought might be acquiescence but when she spoke he learned she had yet another angle.

"I'll level with you, Max. I'm in a bit of pickle.

See, I inherited Isaac as a client and with him came the opportunities his former agent had lined up. There was a miscommunication between him and Isaac that I didn't know about. I promised Citizen the ad assuming Isaac had previously agreed. He hadn't. Isaac said he'd rather focus on his craft instead of marketing."

"That's new," Max grumbled against the rim of his mug. Isaac used to be Mr. Marketing. Probably because he had the acting thing in the bag. Max was less talented in that arena, and not afraid to admit it. He could smile and charm his way through any commercial or photo shoot, but for him, acting on stage was like riding a unicycle and juggling tenpins at the same time. In other words: awkward.

"Don't get me wrong, I'm glad he's focused," she continued. "He told me he'd fly back and film the ad if he could. I'm sure he wouldn't mind you stepping in to help him out."

"So he doesn't know you're here?"

She ignored that interjection, as well. "Plus, you'd be supporting the rest of the cast with a boost in ratings. Think of this gig as a big hug from you to your former TV family."

She had him there. He had a lot of love for the actors on the show. He hadn't been bitter toward any of the cast and crew at the end, just Isaac, who had forced Max into one too many corners after the show had ended.

"A big hug from Isaac you mean," he corrected.

"Since we wouldn't be telling anyone it was me in the commercial."

"Yes, I suppose you're right." A delicate pleat formed between her dark eyebrows. "If you're worried about passing as Isaac there are ways around it. Your hair could use a trim, but not much. Isaac wears his in a longish style nowadays."

Max palmed the back of his head. He'd admit there were a few more errant curls tickling his ears than usual, but he didn't like this woman suggesting he "trim" his carelessly wavy hair. Not one bit.

"The beard will have to go, but it'll grow right back. I promise."

His hand froze in his hair and he narrowed his eyes in warning. No way, no how was he shaving his beard.

"Your expenses to LA and back will be covered by the agency, and I'll remit payment to you personally if you like. Just as soon as Citizen sends it."

He rose from his chair, seeing red and now thoroughly sick of this one-sided conversation. She was assuming an awful lot, especially since she refused to accept no for an answer. He'd been steamrolled one too many times in his life, and as much as he hated to break it to California, she didn't quite carry the weight to press him flat.

"Max?"

Before he allowed her warm brown gaze to seep into his soul, he issued one final warning. "Ms. Squire, it's time for you to leave."

Three

Kendall, her eyes turned up at a seething Max Dunn, shut her mouth with a click. He was telling her no. Like a real no.

"Max—"

"I didn't see any chains on your tires."

"Uh—" Okay. Was the phrase a metaphor she hadn't heard before? "Chains?"

"Yeah. Chains for scooting your way out of my driveway and down the mountain."

"I'm staying at a hotel in downtown Dunn. It's close by, right?"

"Sure. Winding twists and turns and a cliff-side drop-off. Right down the road." His smile held no humor.

"Well. I should be on my way, then." She walked

to the front door and stuffed her feet into her boots, bracing herself for the snowy walkway again. "If we could meet for coffee tomorrow, I can tell you the details of—eep!"

The little screech exited her throat as she turned to find Max *right there*, standing over her, looking even less pleased than he had a few seconds ago.

"I'm going to say this one more time, and only because I respect what you do for a living."

"You do?" She was shocked he felt anything but animosity for a woman who represented the town he hated.

"My answer is no. I am not flying to LA to do a commercial for Citizen watches. I don't want the money. I don't want the watches. I don't want to act any longer. Don't bring my brother or the cast into this discussion again. It's a low blow, meant to play on my emotions and make me say yes out of some sort of misplaced guilt or need to please." He leaned a touch closer, dousing her in his clean, cedar scent. "Know this, California. I suffer from neither guilt nor the need to please. You're wasting your time trying to convince me."

He jerked open the door where the snow fell in a seemingly white sheet beyond the covered porch.

"Drive safe."

Kendall stomped outside, ignoring the chill as she waded through the snow. Once she was in her rental car, she fired up the heater and muttered a frustrated litany to herself.

"He is impossible!" She rubbed her hands together

furiously to warm them, figuring her temper would also help bring up her body temperature. "Stubborn mountain man. What does he have to do that is more important than helping his own family? I'd do it for my brother in a heartbeat."

Ignoring the surge of emotion that arrived with thoughts of Quin, she reversed the car, attempted to peel out and spun the back tires. She took a breath, eased her foot onto the gas and, this time, made it onto the road. Max was standing in his doorway, probably scowling.

"I've got this, you Neanderthal," she grumbled as she drove away—carefully. She kept her hands at the ten o'clock and two o'clock positions on the steering wheel as she traversed the slick, snowy road. She tried not to think of the cliff-side drop-off Max had casually mentioned. "What a jerk."

A delicious, tall, broad, bearded jerk. With fathomless blue eyes and a sexy voice and an undeniable presence. "He would have been perfect for the commercial," she added aloud, mainly to convince herself that her attraction was instead a professional observation. "What a lost opportunity."

Snow pounded her windshield harder as it fell faster—seeming faster still whenever she put her foot on the gas. As a result, she had topped out at a whopping fifteen miles per hour. The GPS claimed that the hotel was five miles down the road but after the misstep with the location of Max's house she didn't trust it. She could be twenty miles away from her hotel for all she knew.

"I'll just use the extra time to come up with a plan," she told herself as she squinted at the white landscape ahead. There had to be another way to film the commercial. Maybe Citizen would agree to fly to the island where Isaac was stranded? Of course, that would mean Isaac sharing the location of the island he was stranded on, which seemed unlikely. She thought back to her videoconference with him at the beginning of the week.

"Isaac. I'm so glad you picked up." It was the fourth time she'd tried and she was beginning to worry she'd never reach him. A backdrop of sand and turquoise sea stood behind her lone client. Isaac looked well, wearing a navy blue T-shirt and mirrored sunglasses. He grinned at the camera and greeted her in kind.

"Hey, Kendall. Sorry for the delay. Reception is spotty out here. Which is why I love it." His grin could sail a thousand ships. Or sell thousands of watches. Which was precisely the reason she needed him back in LA immediately.

"I'm calling about the Citizen ad—" was all she got out before he interrupted.

"An ad I told Lou I wasn't interested in. An ad I told you I wasn't interested in." Impatience crept into his tone, making him sound stern.

She pasted on a brighter smile in the hopes she could outshine his negativity. "Yes, but you did say if you could, you would film it and that's what I'm proposing to you today. I was thinking, since your pilot is unavailable to fly you off your island, I could arrange for a plane to pick you up. You can film the ad in LA and then return to solitude."

"Which would mean disclosing my location. Which I am not doing. There's a reason I'm here and not in my apartment, Kendall."

"Privacy," she said at the same time he did.

The rest of the conversation had been cordial but unsuccessful. If he wasn't going to give up the coordinates to his island, there was no way to bring the film crew for the commercial to him.

She fiddled with the controls on the car's dashboard in an attempt to defog the windshield currently growing more opaque by the second.

"Oh, come on!" She reached up to swipe the glass with her palm, the first swipe making it clear she was on the wrong side of the road. A truck blared its horn and sped past her. With a bleat of panic, she jerked into the correct lane, her heart hammering in her chest.

"Okay, okay," she breathlessly reassured herself as she tightened her hold on the wheel with cold yet sweaty palms. "Okay."

Just as she blew out a steadying breath, the GPS instructed her to turn left. She didn't see a road, but maybe there was one at the opening up ahead? Navigating through the thick snow, and watching for oncoming traffic, she approached the opening as GPS repeated its command to "turn left."

Kendall obeyed, and instantly knew she'd made a huge mistake.

The tires bumped along the "road," which was

instead a path in the woods. Thick tree branches swatted the car windows as tall grass tangled around the tires. She tapped the brakes, but the car skidded rather than slowed, moving at a decent clip along the forest floor. Just as she was picturing careening over the edge of the mountain and dying in a fiery crash, the front of the car bonked into a thick tree trunk with a *crunch*. She was definitely going to have to pay for that when she returned this baby to the rental car facility.

"Okay, okay," she repeated even though the mantra hadn't calmed her nerves the first time around. "You've got this."

When she turned the key, the engine caught, heat blowing from the vents once again. She laughed. "Yes! I knew it."

Putting the car in Reverse, she gently depressed the gas pedal…and went nowhere at all. She pressed harder, hearing the tires spin in the snow, but still nothing. Without traction—*or chains, dammit*—she wasn't going anywhere.

"You have arrived at your destination," the GPS proclaimed. She punched the off button with one finger and swore. Now what?

In another circumstance the winter wonderland surrounding her would have been beautiful. Nothing but snow-covered pine branches as far as the eye could see. Well, aside of the fat tree trunk blocking her view. Twisting in her seat, she turned and spotted the road behind her, within walking distance—thank God. All she had to do was make it to the road, walk in the direction of the hotel, and flag down the next vehicle heading in or out of town.

Piece of cake.

Her smile faded as she realized she had no idea where the hotel was, or where she was. She picked up her phone and powered it on. She'd call for help. The signal was weak out here, but maybe she could get through…

After three failed attempts to connect a call, she gave up. The car's engine dying and the vents halting was all it took for her to panic. Repeating to herself that she had this, she unzipped her suitcase in the back seat and dug out a pair of socks. They were thin, but better than braving the elements barefoot. No matter how silly they looked showing through her fashionable shoes, she was wearing them. She also grabbed a sweater and tugged it over her shirt and leather jacket. She was uncomfortable and overstuffed, but hopefully she would be warm. She tugged on the socks, pulled on her boots and climbed out into ankle-deep snow.

It didn't take long for the cold to sink into her bones.

Neither did a car happen by.

She'd opted to walk in the direction of Max's house, given she had no idea where "town" was and couldn't risk dying out here. She was only so stubborn.

By the time his house came into view, she was beginning to think the dying part would happen anyway. Her limbs were wooden, she couldn't feel her toes. She had no idea how long she'd been climbing the snowy road. Her phone had given up on her entirely, offering only a black screen when she checked again to see if she had any bars. Her hands, one locked around her purse strap, the other tucked into the sleeve of her sweater, were tight and cramping from the cold.

"Almost th-there," she said through chattering teeth. Max's cozy cabin with an orange glow in the windows beckoned her forward but seemed miles away instead of mere yards. Surely she wouldn't keel over on his doorstep. Though, she thought with a frozen smile, it'd serve him right for sending her out in this weather.

That was her last thought before she saw his front door fly open. She swore it was a mirage coming at her, but no, it was Max. In his flannel button-down, no coat, jogging toward her in boots with the laces untied. She opened her mouth to tell him not to trip, but her tongue felt as frozen as her fingers. By the time he reached her, his scowl was scowling and his breath was exiting his beard in hard, visible puffs.

"What the hell, California?" he growled. A second later she was off her feet and in his arms. She buried her freezing nose against his neck and inhaled his cedar-and-smoke scent. The heat emanating off him was reminiscent of a cozy fire. She hummed and attempted to snuggle closer, but her purse was in the way. That was taken from her as well, and paired with another low grumble from her rescuer.

Four

The tow truck's fat cable cranked and spun, dragging California's rental car from its snowy entrapment in the thicket and out onto the equally snowy road.

Max, his arms folded over a thick Carhartt jacket, was braced against the cold air out of habit—he wasn't cold. He had his simmering rage to keep him warm.

"She walked to your house?" Luca asked. Luca O'Hare owned and operated a company in Dunn providing tows and salt trucks to the mountain-bound locals. He was a godsend in weather like this, keeping the roads safe and dragging more than one sunny-Cali visitor's wheels out of the snow.

"Yeah."

Luca shook his head. "Damn."

Damn just about covered it. Though Max could think of a few less decent swear words to add to the mix. Not directed at Kendall, who hadn't known what she was getting into, taking off for the hotel in this snowstorm, but at himself. He'd known better than to let her leave his house in these conditions.

"Where's she staying?" Luca asked as he secured her car for the tow to the garage.

"In town."

Luca shook his head. "She won't make it."

"You're right about that." Max had let her walk out of his house once, but he wouldn't let her do it again.

"She pretty?" Luca smiled around a thick, black goatee. He was swarthier than Max, which was saying something. Luca's hair, wedged under a knit hat, was equally thick. He shoved his black-rimmed glasses higher on his nose.

"She's thawing out in front of my fireplace."

Luca's grin widened. "So, she's *very* pretty."

"Call me when it's ready," Max said rather than answer that yes, Kendall Squire was *very* pretty. She was also *very* stubborn, *very* focused and *very* unprepared for life in the mountains.

"Will do." Luca maneuvered down the mountain as Max drove his truck back to his cabin. The chimney puffed smoke from the fireplace and his gut instantly unraveled from the knot it'd been in since he spotted Kendall shuffling up the road looking like a ghost. If he hadn't happened to step outside to grab a few more logs for the fireplace, he hated to think what could have happened.

When he'd taken her into his house, she'd had her nose and mouth buried in the crook of his neck and was mumbling something about how he smelled like a cozy fire. He'd muttered back that she'd be warm soon enough, and for once she hadn't argued with him.

Inside, he spotted her in the same place where he'd left her, snuggled beneath two thick blankets on the couch. She was facing the fireplace, eyes shut, likely fast asleep.

He blew out another breath of relief that she was safe in his warm house instead of freezing into a solid block of ice outside it.

He lowered his ass onto the couch cushion next to her and she stirred, but her eyes remained shut. He gave her one more good tuck, pulling the blankets over her sock-covered feet. He'd given her a pair of his wool socks after the fire was going. The thin excuse for socks she had worn while walking most of the way here wasn't suited for a spring day let alone a snowstorm.

Max had built this cabin in the mountains years ago. Not himself, but he'd been heavily involved with the contractors out here, visiting almost daily to ensure it matched his vision. After spending years in LA, he knew what he wanted, and it wasn't a modern glass shrine overlooking the Hollywood hills. He didn't want neighbors. He didn't want fancy, overpriced grocery stores. He wanted solace. The peace that had eluded him while he'd been growing up in front of a live studio audience.

Isaac loved every moment of time spent in Hollywood. Attending school in the studio or in their shared trailer rather than going to actual class, being recognized whenever they were out with their parents at a restaurant or spotted at the beach by fans. Max felt the opposite. He'd have much rather been at school or throwing a football on Friday night. And he preferred to finish a meal rather than stop halfway through his burger to sign an autograph.

He wasn't trying to sound ungrateful. *Brooks Knows Best* afforded him many privileges while he was growing up, and now. But he was finished with that part of his life. When he'd first heard the show was reuniting, he'd had mixed emotions. First, he thought "good for them" but soon after came the thought "I'm not doing a reunion show."

Isaac had asked. Carefully, but he had asked. He'd wanted to bring Max "along for the ride" and assured him he wouldn't have to do anything other than a walk-on as an extra character. The fans of the show would love to see him, Isaac had promised, and Max wouldn't have to commit to a full schedule since Isaac was playing Danny Brooks alone.

Max's knee-jerk reaction had been a hard no—as hard a no as he'd given Kendall Squire when she'd asked him to star in an ad. He came to these mountains to be alone. He was forced into fame, or maybe *coerced* was a better word for it, by his parents and later by his starstruck brother. Now was Max's time.

He wanted to live the way he wanted to live and that didn't involve stepping in front of a camera.

A rare wave of remorse rolled over him as he watched Kendall sleep. His distaste for performing shouldn't have clouded his judgment. He never should have let her walk out his door. But, hell, what was he supposed to do, tell her she wasn't allowed to leave? He doubted she would have listened. But he could have offered to follow her down the hill in his truck to ensure she arrived safely in town.

"Max?" Kendall's eyes were still closed, her lips pursed softly.

"Yeah, California, it's me."

She was not only plucky but tough as nails. If he wasn't so pissed off at himself, he might smile at her persistence.

Her eyelashes fluttered and then her dark gaze landed on him. "I'm going to need a ride."

Kendall, feeling groggy, but oh-so-warm buried in Max's blankets and wearing his socks, looked up at her host hopefully. She'd felt him settle in next to her, tuck her in tight. It wasn't hard to guess what he was thinking. That she was a clueless Californian who attempted to drive on an ice skating rink without chains on her tires.

As much as she didn't want to move a single stiff limb on her body, she intended to relocate to her hotel room and leave his cabin as soon as possible. Unfortunately, that would involve him giving her a ride to town since she no longer had an operational vehicle.

"You're not going anywhere." His low voice was oddly soothing.

"You live in the mountains. Don't you have a truck?"

"A big one," he answered.

"I assume you can drive in this mess." Since he didn't respond, she continued. "I have reservations at M Hotel."

"You're going to have to cancel those."

"I can't *cancel* them."

He turned his head to look out the back window. Fat snowflakes fell in a white waterfall, inches of the stuff lining the sills. She took her eyes off the frosty wonderland to focus on Max.

His profile was ridiculously attractive. Lines fanned out at the corners of his eyes, reminding her he was far from the boy he used to play on TV. He was also far from having glycolic peels on the regular. It was refreshing to look at a man who wasn't as polished, whitened or smooth as the men she typically saw in California.

"Second thought," he told her, "You probably won't have to cancel. They won't be expecting you to show in this mess."

"I have to." She righted herself, pushing out of her blanket cocoon. "What am I supposed to do? Sleep here?" The reality of her situation hit her suddenly. Now that she wasn't freezing to death her brain had kicked into high gear. "I left my bag in the car. I need my things." She threw the blankets off, but when she moved to stand, her head swam. She put a palm to her forehead and sat down again.

"Easy, California. Your bag's in my room. Your car's at the shop. Your person is staying right where you are until you climb the stairs and sleep in my bed."

Her belly dropped, a delicious sensation both full and fluttery. Hearing him command her to sleep in his bed ticked several boxes in the attributes of her fantasy guy. Which made no sense. She didn't like Max. Not like that.

"I, uh, I need to get to the hotel, Max." Especially since the attraction she felt when she'd first knocked on his front door hadn't gone anywhere. This was beyond inconvenient.

"You could have been killed." A shadow darkened his brow. "You had no business attempting that drive, and as much as I'd like to fulfill your request and keep my bed to myself tonight, I also have no business driving in a snowstorm."

She let the reference to his bed bounce around her head for a second before she reminded him his truck had chains on the tires.

"Chains or no. I'm not risking you being caught out in the elements again. You need to rest and stay warm. Do you want tea?"

His gruff voice was firm and unyielding, yet beyond the gravel, she heard something else. Care. Max cared about her enough to keep her safe and warm. That made her think of her brother Quin. The way he used to look out for her. She'd felt safe and protected with him, too. And maybe because today was his birthday, or simply because she was tired and comfortable, she snuggled into the blankets and nodded her agreement.

Max stood and went to the kitchen to prepare her tea. She watched him move around the space, fill the kettle with water, open a drawer and pull out a spoon, take a jar of honey from the cabinet. If asked when she'd first laid eyes on him, she would have said he was as far from domestic as she was. Kendall was more likely to drop by a juice bar or a coffee shop and order a drink than to putter around in the kitchen making it. There was an almost homey quality about him. It was jarring, and didn't fit her earlier assumptions.

But then, the same could be said about her, couldn't it? Since she was a little girl, she couldn't fathom the idea of a "normal" job. Fetching coffee and answering emails for Lou had been more invigorating than when she'd worked anywhere else.

Kendall loved the limelight. Not for herself, but as an industry. She loved matching clients with their dream roles, and watching television shows and movies come to fruition. Before Lou retired, he was very involved in his clients' lives. He'd help them rehearse and meet face-to-face whenever possible. She'd looked up to Lou, still did, even though he'd left without much warning. Just enough to allow her time to buy a cake and gather the agency staff for a fond farewell.

Taking his place had proved harder than she'd

imagined. She'd tried not to feel hurt when client after client fired her. She'd called Lou for consolation and he'd lent an ear, but he'd quickly and pragmatically told her it'd be up to her to foster relationships and make her own way in this business. She'd never forget his advice. "Tenacity is a requirement, Kendall."

It was tenacity that made her persevere when Isaac couldn't do the Citizen commercial. Tenacity that brought her to Max's doorstep to make him an offer she swore not to let him refuse. Tenacity that had her reaching for her cell phone on the coffee table. A cord restricted its movement, and as she was reaching to unhook the phone from the charger, Max set a mug of hot tea in front of her.

"I'd recommend you slow down while you're here," he told her. Then he settled in a chair across from her, his eyes on her hand wrapped around her cell phone.

"I'm here to work. Did you think this was a vacation for me?"

Blue eyes perused her face in a leisurely manner before he shook his head back and forth deliberately. "No. I s'pose I didn't."

Five

Kendall, her eyes on his, traded her cell phone for her mug. Steam rolled off the top of the cup and disappeared into the long, wavy hair framing her face. Luca was right in his guess that her face was pretty, but wrong about the *very*. Max would go as far as to say she was extremely pretty, or hell, gorgeous, if a man could still call a woman that. She had legs to die for; shrewd yet kind brown eyes; and a forged-in-iron attitude impossible not to admire.

If asked to describe the perfect woman, he'd have mentioned tall, intelligent and blond. The blond in Kendall's hair was highlights in chestnut brown, a far cry from his ex-wife's lighter blond hair. Bunny was also shorter, and while she could match Kendall for her stubbornness, he had the idea California would win in a match of wits.

"The couch is fine, by the way," she told him. "Or a guest bedroom. You don't have to offer your own bed."

"I do if the guest rooms upstairs don't have beds. Plus, guessing you don't want to be woken up at five in the morning when I make my coffee. I'll take the couch."

She argued she could handle an early wake up call, and then he reminded her that five a.m. here was two a.m. in California.

"I know." She lifted her chin, daring him to challenge her further.

"You're argumentative, anyone ever tell you that?" He laughed before lifting his own mug of tea to his lips, but didn't so much as take a sip before she argued with him again.

"I'm tenacious. It's a requirement in my business." She took a breath but didn't speak, instead chewing on her lip. He guessed she was thinking of what to say to convince him to film the commercial. If she asked him again, he'd have to be firmer than he was before, and he wasn't looking forward to that. Not so soon after her trauma this evening.

"Where's your room?" she asked, once again throwing him off. Hell, was it so surprising he didn't know what she was thinking? His two-year marriage to Bunny had proved he had no business living with a woman.

"Upstairs, turn left. Last door at the end of the

hall." She set her mug down and started to push off the couch when he asked, "Going to bed already?"

"I'm going to get my suitcase."

"No. You're not." He set his mug next to hers and stood. She lowered to the couch but kept her eyes on him. "You're going to sit there and drink your tea. I'll get it for you."

"It's not heavy, Max. I can carry it."

"Kendall. Let me." He leaned over her, watching as the stubborn shot out of her eyes and was replaced with acquiescence. It was a beautiful sight. Not because she was letting him have his way, but because what he saw in her expression was trust. Trust, he liked. "Be right back."

As he climbed the stairs to fetch her bag, he figured trust was a rare find in her business. It was hard to rely on someone when money talked. As he'd learned from his parents, who had worked in the industry for years in some capacity. His father was a director, his mom a former actress, though she'd never achieved the success her sons had. Once his face appeared on merchandise, it became harder for Max to wrap his head around what success meant.

Though, to be fair, he had shared his face with Isaac his whole life. After staring into a face identical to his for so long, lending his likeness to a board game or a T-shirt wasn't so odd after all.

Once he and Isaac had had their final falling-out, Max let him and their parents know he'd be leaving California for the East Coast. His parents had tried to argue, but in the end had been more understanding than his brother. Isaac looked out for himself first. As proved by him absconding to a private island when he should have stayed close to home. What if the show's producer needed to have a sit-down with him? What if there was a last-minute promotional opportunity—like the one Kendall needed him for?

Max shook his head, reminding himself that Isaac's career wasn't any of his business. Not anymore. Just the way he liked it.

He delivered Kendall's suitcase to her feet, and she bent forward to unzip a compartment and pull out a laptop. He watched her fingers fly over the keys, observed the subtle way she flinched whenever she read something on the screen before those fingers flew again.

"You planning on resting while you're here?" he asked, half-amused.

"I'm planning," she said, her eyes on the screen rather than him, "on catching up with email so I can clear my head for more important thinking."

He'd called it, hadn't he? Smart.

"There has to be a way to shoot a Citizen commercial without Isaac. I just haven't figured out how yet."

Other than my pretending to be Isaac, he thought but didn't say.

"Why not let it go? There will be other sponsors. Isaac's middle name is marketing. He'll bounce back. Clearly he wasn't worried about being at home since he absconded to Belle Island."

Her head snapped up, her eyes widening along with her smile. "He's on Belle Island?"

"Oh, shit. Don't—forget I said that."

Her face lit with excitement. "I can fly the film crew to him, Max. All I have to do is get him to agree. He wouldn't tell me where he was before, but now that I know I can figure out distance and how long it'll take to fly down and back. He did say he'd do it if he were in the States. Why wouldn't he if I went to him?" While she talked, her fingers moved over the keyboard again.

"Kendall—"

"It's going to work," she mumbled to herself. And since he had about a zero percent chance of rerouting her attention from her task, he decided to leave her to it.

Clearly, she wasn't interested in resting or recuperating. She might be incapable of it. A trait that made Kendall Squire instantly undesirable—despite her beauty or her smarts or her tenacity.

Hustle culture could kiss his ass. There were more important things in life than climbing Success Mountain.

At the window, he watched the snow fall gracefully in the distance. It clung to trees and piled high on the ground. He sucked in a breath as a smile pulled his cheeks. Yes, there were more important things in life than success. He was grateful he'd found his slice of paradise away from the rat race.

Kendall stopped typing the email to Isaac when she heard the back door pop open. She looked up to see Max step outside onto a wide, covered patio. He passed the door and stood in front of a pair of large windows nearest her. There, he stopped and lifted the lid off a hot tub. Steam rose from the vessel and swirled around him, making him look like a magic genie come to grant her three wishes.

For my first wish, how about you agree to do your brother's Citizen commercial?

With a sigh, she abandoned the email she'd been drafting and, before she talked herself out of it, called Isaac. Not on video, though. She didn't need him to know she was trapped at his brother's house. How would she explain being *here*?

"Kendall, hi," he shouted over music. The volume cranked down a second later. "Sorry. I was working out. What's up?"

"You're on Belle Island," she blurted out. "It's a six-and-a-half-hour flight from California. I can have the film crew on your back porch by tomorrow afternoon. Evening at the latest. The shoot will probably take two hours. Your costar is a model who has done commercial spots before, so she's a pro. I won't be able to make it, but you can handle it without me, right?"

Silence.

"Isaac?"

"How do you know where I am?" His voice was low and growly, reminding her of Max. She'd never heard Isaac sound growly before.

"Your brother didn't mean to, but he mentioned where you were."

"You called Max?"

"I talked to him," she said, because *no*, she hadn't

called him. She'd shown up on his doorstep, left defeated, and then nearly died of hypothermia on his driveway. "What's the big deal?"

"The big deal, Kendall," Isaac continued gruffly, "is Danny Brooks."

"The big deal is your character from the show?"

"It's the role that made Isaac Dunn relevant. The role continues to be the one people remember me for most. Playing Danny is a twenty-year journey into the past. I can't screw it up. I can't show up and say *the line* wrong. Could you imagine?"

His voice had taken on a panicky quality. She knew the role was important to him. Sitcom or no, the show had a loyal fan following. Fans asked Isaac to do *the line* quite often, and he'd almost always obliged.

"Isaac, you've been saying that line to anyone who approached you on the street and asked since the show wrapped. You're not going to screw it up."

"I can't risk it," he said.

"Come on, say it."

"No."

"Isaac."

His silence reminded her of Max's stoicism, but unlike his twin brother, Isaac gave in.

"Give me a break," he said, the emphasis on *give*, dragging out the *br* in break.

Nailed it.

"*You're* what fans want," she told him with a smile. "It's not the line, but the way you say it that makes it iconic." She pressed the phone to her cheek. "You *are* Danny, Isaac. What's there to prepare?"

She expected to hear her client's smile through the phone, and hear a "yeah, you're right" before he agreed to film the Citizen ad after all. She'd still have to talk Citizen into flying the film crew to Belle Island, but hey, one step at a time. Tenacity! Just as she was plotting her next phone call, Isaac surprised her once again. She didn't hear his smile through the phone, but the cry of seagulls on the ocean air. And he didn't say "yeah you're right" and agree to do the commercial, either.

Instead, he said, "I'm only half Danny, Kendall. The other half is my brother, who, by the way, was the one who said *the line* the way it is now. I'd always argued we should say *gimme a break* instead, but the director preferred Max's take on it." Isaac dismissed her and himself with a harsh warning. "You fly a film crew to my island, Kendall, you're fired. And I know you can't afford to lose me."

She blew out the words, "Isaac, wait" but it was too late. He'd already ended the call.

The patio door shut behind Max as he let himself inside. Snowflakes dotted his shoulders and stuck to his hair before melting in the warmer air of the cabin. "You okay, California?"

"Perfect," she lied, tossing her cell phone onto the coffee table next to her cooling tea. "Other than your brother threatening to fire me if I set foot on his island. Or the fact that I'm stuck here with you as we are buried in several inches of snow."

"More like several feet," he interjected unhelpfully.

"I'm assuming grabbing a flight out of here first thing in the morning is out of the question."

Even if she'd still believed tenacity and optimism could overcome her circumstance, Max's sharp laugh and head shake would have doused her high hopes.

"That's what I thought." She'd have to call Citizen and admit that wires were crossed when Lou left. She'd agreed to a contract she couldn't fulfill. She'd make Isaac sound like the good guy, which he was, and tell them she respected his boundaries while he prepared to reprise the role of a lifetime. The thought made her cringe. She hadn't respected his boundaries at all. How had she become the kind of person who put her needs before everyone else's?

Heat hit the backs of her eyes and her nose tingled. She willed the tears back, clearing her throat deliberately as she grabbed her laptop. She was just tired.

"I'll figure something out," she said more for her own benefit than Max's. "I'll be working late. You might as well let me take the couch." She stared him down, his face so handsome it was stupefying. She pictured Isaac with his clean-shaven jaw and slightly slimmer build, perfect dark hair styled against his head, short in the back, long and wavy top. Max's was more of an all-over-in-need-of-a-trim, but it really worked for him.

Assuming her telling him she was sleeping on the couch would fall silent on his, oddly enough, *attractive* ears, she readied her next argument.

"Suit yourself," he said, trapping the prepared argument in her throat.

At least it kept the tears of defeat at bay. That's the reason she told herself she'd nearly cried, but it wasn't. It was Quinton's voice in her head that had nearly brought her to tears. When she was sixteen years old he'd told her she could be anyone she wanted to be. That she was a natural leader. That the world would take notice the moment she was wheels down in LAX. "Kendall Squire," he'd told her, "is going to run Tinsel Town."

She'd believed him when he'd painted the picture of her swimming in a sea of success, and he'd been wrong. But then, she'd also believed him when he went on a hiking trip with his two best friends and promised to come home in three days' time.

He'd been wrong about that, too.

Six

Max's eyes opened at four fifty-five in the morning, his usual time. Try as he might, he couldn't sleep late no matter what time he went to bed at night.

He'd left Kendall on the sofa, still pecking at her laptop at 10:00 p.m., but he hadn't fallen asleep right away. He heard her voice well after midnight. It carried up the stairs and bounced off the high ceilings. He hadn't been able to make out the words, but her soft, tinkling laughter and gentle, reassuring cadence had eventually lulled him to sleep.

He was starting to have sympathy for the woman. Max could have warned her his brother wouldn't be receptive to a film crew on his island, but he was learning she was the type of person who had to see for herself.

An admirable quality...until it was used on him.

Dressed in thick socks, jeans and a flannel and tee, he padded down the stairs and passed a pile of blankets on the couch. If he hadn't spotted a tangle of hair peeking out of those blankets, he'd have assumed Kendall was already up and at 'em.

Her laptop was open, the screen black, the cord plugged into the side. Her cell phone was nowhere to be seen, though it wouldn't have surprised him to learn she'd slept with it in her hand. Her suitcase was open, an array of unsuitable clothing inside. Amongst the frilly, floral and thin garments were several pairs of spiky shoes. Other than the sweater she'd pulled on to walk to his house, he wondered if she owned anything warm enough for this visit.

He felt a ping of irritation that she'd slept down here instead of taking his bed. Tonight, he'd convince her to let him sleep on the couch.

He put the coffeepot on and stepped outside onto the patio. There, he folded his arms over his chest and breathed in the crisp, cold air. Snow fell silently, though slower than before. It hadn't stopped during the night. No way was California catching a plane out of Virginia today. If she hadn't regretted this fruitless trip before, he was sure she would when he told her the bad news.

The cold cut through his flannel shirt and Henley, so he turned and went inside. He found Kendall in the kitchen wrapped head to toe in a bulky blanket.

"Morning," he said, interrupting her staring contest with the coffeepot.

She looked sleepy. A tad out of sorts. He figured after the flight, the drive, the accident and the subsequent hike yesterday, she very well was.

"How do you feel?"

She rolled a shoulder from beneath the blanket and shrugged with her mouth. "A little sore. Kind of achy. Nothing coffee won't fix."

"You'd better take it easy just in case," he warned, his shoulders stiffening. If she came down with a cold because of yesterday, he'd never forgive himself.

"Can you check on my car? I need to schedule a flight. I'm hoping to be out of your hair by this afternoon."

He pulled two mugs from the cabinet in front of her and filled them both with coffee. "Hate to break it to you, California, but you're going to be here at least through the weekend."

"But it's Thursday." The whine in her voice should have set his teeth on edge. For some reason he thought it was cute. Maybe because she was still wrapped in his bedding, or because her hair was rumpled in a sexy way, or hell, maybe because he hadn't had anyone in his house to take care of in a long time. He'd sought out privacy and seclusion, hell, had prioritized it, but on days like this with nothing on the agenda and snow falling outside the windows, being alone was…well, *lonely*.

"You're sleeping in my bed tonight. As you've noticed, it's chilly downstairs unless you hop up and stoke the fire every so often."

She shuffled past him to the fridge and returned with a container of flavored coffee creamer. "Didn't peg you for a caramel pecan guy."

"You mean you didn't peg me as sweet." After she poured a dollop into her mug, he did the same.

"I suspect you're in no danger of being accused of sweet." Her forehead crinkled as she lifted her mug to her lips. "Although, if word got out you carried me into your cabin, wrapped me in blankets and loaned me your socks, that rumor might gain traction."

"That was heroic. Not sweet." He'd leaned forward to correct her, stepping closer for no other reason than he liked being near her. He'd liked when she was standing in his doorway arguing with him, too. The moment he'd caught her scent, he'd wanted more. That same familiar scent wafted off her lips now. "Peppermint. That's what you smell like."

Her lips formed a little O, drawing his attention to her mouth. "Lip balm."

He made a sound halfway between a grunt and a growl before he tore his gaze from her lips to refocus on her face. No matter how badly he wanted to find out if she tasted of peppermint, too, he'd do well to keep his focus on what was going on here. She'd ended up in his house against her will because she'd asked him to do something against his. The sooner she was out of his cabin and on her way to California, the sooner he could return to his regularly scheduled life. He'd had enough upsets for a lifetime.

"I'll call Luca about your car," he said. "If you're lucky you won't be stuck here the whole weekend."

* * *

Kendall spent the rest of the morning splitting her attention between the weather report on TV and her laptop. Max had reminded her she wasn't going to "hear anything different no matter how many times you check" but she'd ignored him. He'd gone from looking at her like he wanted to ravish her in the morning to scowling at her like she was an intruder by afternoon.

In a way, she was an intruder. She hadn't been invited here and now he was stuck with her. She'd called the hotel in town to cancel her reservations, but as Max had predicted, they'd guessed she was caught in the weather. She promised to check in as soon as she was able, but they didn't require reservations this time. As Betsy at the front desk had said, "No one is leaving or coming into Dunn for the foreseeable future."

After that phone call, she turned off the television. The weatherman was guessing. Betsy *knew*.

Around lunchtime she moved her things to Max's bedroom and showered and dressed for the day. Slower than she would have preferred, but she hadn't been lying about being achy. Even though the accident had been a small one, she felt the trauma in her bones.

By the time she emerged and walked downstairs, the most heavenly scent was wafting from the direction of the kitchen. Max stood in front of the stove, stirring a pot.

"Chili," he announced.

Her stomach roared. She'd only had coffee for breakfast, so she was starving. They set the table, her pulling out every possible chili topping she found in his fridge—sliced red onion and jalapeño peppers, sharp cheddar cheese and sour cream. No avocado, which was a crime. She pointed that out as he ladled their soup into bowls. Max chuckled. The sound was as hearty as the meal, and she couldn't help humming in pleasure every time she ate a bite.

"I haven't had chili in years."

"Now that's criminal," he said with such seriousness she had to smile.

"It's seventy-three degrees and sunny in LA. Not exactly chili weather."

He scooped up another big bite and chewed thoughtfully, his blue eyes landing on hers and making her feel…she didn't know. *Something.* Not uncomfortable. More aware. That awareness kicked up heat in her cheeks. Heat she couldn't blame on the spice in her lunch.

"Did you always want to be an agent to the stars?" His voice was steady, but she wondered if he meant that ironically. How funny it must have been for him to be "a star" when he was so young.

"I wanted to work in Hollywood, behind the scenes. I used to dream of winning an Oscar the awards show rushed through announcing. You know, the costume designers, the sound producers."

"That's rare. Most people who live in LA want as much attention on them as possible."

"You didn't." She was understanding that about

him. Fame hadn't altered what was important to Max. He was refusing her what she needed, which, yes, was mildly irritating, but he also wasn't willing to compromise. It was admirable. Inconvenient for her purposes, but admirable.

"I had my moments. I was lost in it the same way most famous people are."

"The way you think Isaac is lost in it."

Max blew out a gusty sigh before taking a long drink from the water glass next to him. She was treading on sacred ground, but she couldn't help herself. She was curious about how they'd gone from playing the same person on a sitcom to barely speaking to each other.

"I love my brother. I don't love Hollywood. There's a big difference."

Which was no answer at all.

"I understand how your life isn't there any longer, but didn't a small part of you want to return to the show? To visit the friends you had to have made during the decade you filmed together?" She held up a palm to hopefully keep Max from blowing up. He was glaring at her, his spoon hovering over his bowl. "I know you told me not to play on your emotions. That's not what I'm doing. I've given up trying to convince you to do the commercial."

He blinked, obviously surprised by her confession. She was a bit surprised by it too. Her never-say-die attitude must have frozen to death in the Virginia mountains.

"I would think a walk-on role might be novel for you."

"For a washed-up former child star?"

"You're not washed up. The public is curious about you. They find you mysterious."

"Who thinks I'm mysterious?" One dark eyebrow craned into his disheveled hair.

"My sister, for one. She's a podcaster. The topic is television shows we grew up watching. Guess which show was her favorite?"

"Brooks Knows Best." He shoveled the remainder of the chili into his mouth.

"Yep. She would lose her mind if she knew I was trapped with the one and only Max Dunn. She nearly lost her mind when she found out I was working for Lou, Isaac's former agent—"

"And mine."

"Yours?" Lou had never mentioned he'd represented Max, too.

"I burned bridges when I left." He didn't sound regretful. More contemplative. "I wasn't planning on coming back anyway. Besides, as you well know," he said as he stood from the table to refill his bowl, "if the money's right, personal feelings wouldn't keep a deal from being signed. This is a business."

"Not to me." Her agenting career had always been personal for her. And when her clients had fled from her like she was emitting a noxious gas, she'd taken that personally as well.

"Hot tub later, California." He retook his chair and piled toppings onto his chili. "It'll help."

He must have noticed her shifting uncomfortably in her chair. So much for the idea of him not caring for other people. She could tell Max cared about everyone. Even the agent from California who'd rendered herself snowbound in his private cabin.

Seven

By evening, the Wi-Fi blinked out in the cabin and it took everything within her not to rave like a committed lunatic. She'd been in the middle of replying to an email to the production company for Citizen's upcoming commercial. She typed out how there'd been a "scheduling snafu" with the commercial and asked if they could postpone the shoot. She didn't have high hopes for a postponement. The production company was one of the highest in demand in the industry. But it wouldn't hurt to ask.

"Thanks, Luca." Max strolled into the living room, his cell phone to his ear. "Yeah. I'll tell her." Then he pocketed his phone and stared at her.

Kendall, perched on the edge of the couch cushion, laptop open to her calendar, couldn't take the suspense. "Tell me the prognosis quickly. I'm already sans Wi-Fi, Citizen is going to strangle me when I pull the plug on the commercial, and Isaac is an inch away from firing me. If Luca said it'd be cheaper for me to purchase the rental car than repair it, I wouldn't be the least bit surprised."

Max smiled in such a warm way, it jerked her from her hectic thoughts. He came to where she sat and lowered onto the couch in between her and the neatly folded blankets she'd slept under. "You know, what's on the other side of this hustle only looks like success. Achieving won't give you what you want out of life."

It was such a *Zen* statement, and so counter to the loops her brain was running in, she couldn't decide how to react. Finally, she did, and what came out was, "You have no idea what I want out of life."

His smile erased and she regretted her bluntness. But she wouldn't take it back. Not for all the Wi-Fi in the world. It was the truth. Max didn't know her. He didn't know what was important to her. What mattered to her, down in her soul.

"I'm sorry. That was rude."

"My fault," he said. His voice was low and rocky, and this close, she was hit with the smell of cedar and pine again. "I made assumptions about you. I shouldn't do that."

"You smell like the outdoors." What she'd meant to point out was that she'd started the whole assumption thing, but for whatever reason her mouth usurped her brain's plans.

"Good, I hope." His lips slid to one side. "The outdoors can smell like a lot of different things."

"Very good," she whispered and for whatever reason followed with, "The rest of you is scraggly, but your beard's a work of art." Which took her gaze straight to the firm lips nestled beneath his neat beard. "I mean, I can understand why I upset you by suggesting you shave it."

"I thought you didn't like it." He cocked his head, playfulness leaking into his expression. She'd never suspected he could achieve anything as lighthearted as playful, but here they were.

"I like it."

His blue eyes darkened to navy and he leaned a touch closer. Close enough to engulf her in his definitely good outdoor smell. Close enough for her to forget her place or her mind. The thoughts in her head were no longer focused on her schedule or the lack of internet connection, but on how long it'd been since she'd been kissed.

Too long.

An inch from ending her personal drought, he sat back and shook off whatever haze of attraction had saturated the air between them.

"If you don't have a swimsuit, I can loan you a T-shirt for the hot tub." He stood so abruptly she found herself staring at the stack of blankets instead of his handsome face. "Once you're submerged and incapable of making calls or sending emails, I'll tell you the news about the car."

"Well, that's not very comforting."

He grinned as he nodded for the stairs. "Go change. I'll grab towels."

* * *

Max was already in the hot tub, water bubbling around his shoulders, when he spotted Kendall through the window. He'd turned off the lights inside, hoping she'd take the hint and leave them off when she came out. It was dark, what little sun that had shone through the snowfall having slipped behind the mountains to turn in for the night.

Kendall tiptoed downstairs barefoot, he presumed wearing a swimsuit. She was wrapped in a dark towel and peering around as guiltily as if she'd broken into the place.

Damn. *Cute*.

He'd nearly kissed her earlier. Despite a lecture to himself about how he wanted life to go back to normal, he still wanted to kiss her.

He wasn't saintly by a long stretch, but he'd had a monk-like sex life during the last year. It was terrifying to think of how little physical contact he'd had. He could only sustain his exaggerated objections about kissing the "enemy" for so long.

By the time he'd shared that he loved his brother, and how he'd burned bridges walking away from Lou and LA, he couldn't relegate Kendall as an enemy any longer. He was sincere when he'd apologized about making assumptions. He'd taken one look at her in his doorway and would have bet the entire town of Dunn on her being a ruthless, do-anything-to-get-what-she-wanted city girl. The more time he spent with her, the more fragile she seemed. Not weak, not vulnerable. More like she was close to giving up on something she wanted very much.

At one point in time he'd wanted the role of Danny Brooks more than anything. It was easy to forget how much he'd enjoyed the role and working with the cast and crew. The fame and, face it, the fortune hadn't been all bad.

Since he'd mentioned he was washed up and she'd told him her sister was a superfan, he'd been thinking back to those days. At age fifteen he'd retired from the show, and by age twenty he was burned out. When he'd walked away, he'd done more than burn bridges. He'd torn them off their cables like Godzilla on a rampage. He'd assumed he'd always feel as betrayed by fame as he had felt back then. And while he'd told Kendall the truth about being through with acting, he had to admit, he couldn't call up the feeling of dread that'd once accompanied talking about his former career.

"*Omigod*, it's freezing out here!" She shut the door behind her and made short work of walking to the hot tub. She stopped abruptly and eyed the plastic steps leading up to the ledge. "Can you close your eyes while I get in? I can't gracefully scale these stairs and swing a leg over."

"Sure you can." He stood from the warm water, steam rolling off his shoulders. Kendall's mouth popped open as her eyes roamed over his bare chest, down to his shorts and back up again. He wasn't the only one suffering from a bout of inconvenient attraction. He offered his hand.

She regarded it briefly. When a gust of icy wind blew beneath the patio, she moved into action. She rested her smaller hand in his, dropped the towel onto a chair he'd set next to the hot tub, and climbed in. Max tried not to stare, honest to God, but he was incapable of tearing his eyes off her dark green bikini. The top clung to small, perky breasts, a bow in the center begging to be unknotted. The bottoms were low-cut and tasteful, but sexy as hell. Or maybe that was her thick thighs. Far from slim and athletic, the flare of her hips was enough to send his imagination straight for the gutter.

By the time he lowered into the water, he was having a stern talking-to with his manhood, which was currently swelling thanks to the sight of his houseguest in as little clothing as he'd ever seen her.

"Incredible," came her husky praise, which didn't diminish the state of his arousal in the least. "We can sit here and watch it snow but be as warm and toasty as when we're inside. Wow."

He rerouted his attention to the snow, falling at a fast clip and adding to the inches blanketing the woods behind his house.

They listened to the soft sound of fat flakes hitting the trees for a few minutes. Until she pointed out a pair of squirrels scurrying over the pine boughs in the distance. He expected her to keep talking about scenery, but instead, she said something he didn't expect.

"My older brother's birthday was yesterday." Her words were weighted, like her brother's birthday wasn't a happy occasion. She proved his theory correct when she added, "He died when I was sixteen."

Before he could apologize for her loss, she went on.

"He was the one who promised I'd achieve everything I wanted in Hollywood. My parents were more pragmatic. They constantly managed my expectations. Protecting me, I guess. They reminded me to get an education and to have a backup plan. Not Quinton." Up to her neck in steamy, bubbly water, she smiled wistfully. "He told me never to let anyone yuck on my yum. That's a direct quote, by the way."

Her smile turned sad and the untethered emotion socked Max square in the chest. He couldn't imagine losing his brother in a permanent sense. Even when they'd been apart, he'd known Isaac was a phone call or a flight away. Once someone died, that was no longer the case.

"For years, I believed him. I imagined sailing through life on a cloud of dreams. I relocated to California and worked my butt off doing anything I could to remain in the industry. I was a prop person. I filled the food cart. I delivered coffee and answered emails. Lou gave me my first real shot. By the time I moved from interning for him to being a paid assistant, I was over the moon. I was almost there...and then Lou left and handed me part of his client list. I was so sure I'd stumbled upon my big break—to use terminology you know well."

She sighed and he felt that in his chest, too. The weighty disappointment of falling short of your own expectations. He'd been there. Nothing was worse than being within reach of what you wanted and failing to attain it. He'd felt that way after the show had wrapped, before Isaac and Lou sentenced Max to five more years of penance.

She turned her head to watch the snow, the line of her graceful neck holding up a chin refusing to turn down. Gaze up and forward, Kendall was a woman who didn't take defeat easily.

"I let my brother down," she concluded before she pinned Max with what could only be described as heartbreaking remorse. "The hustle isn't about success for me, Max. It's about me becoming the person my brother saw in me. He was certain I would make it. And here I am, farther away than when I first landed in LA with no idea what I was getting myself into."

LA was like that. Even though Isaac and Max had lived in California their whole lives, Max would admit he didn't understand Hollywood until he was in the middle of it. Once *Brooks Knows Best* surpassed everyone's expectations of how big the show would become, and Isaac and Max surpassed their own parents' fame, they were on a runaway freight train.

"I wonder if the snowstorm is a sign I've been doing the wrong thing with my life. That's a hard pill to swallow after ten years of hard work."

"Tell me about it," he said, sounding gruff but not for the reason she'd think. Not out of regret for how he'd spent his time. Just out of understanding.

Kendall and he had more in common than he'd originally believed.

"I'm sorry I crashed into your perfectly peaceful life." Her sincerity was killing him. If she'd started with that sentiment the day she'd knocked on his door, he would have agreed. Now, though... Now he didn't.

"What if you shoot the commercial here and send the footage to the film crew?"

She watched him carefully, a beautiful sight with eyes wide over warm, pink cheeks and snow falling gently behind her. "What do you mean?"

"If you film the commercial here, you can send the footage to the film crew. Pitch the idea of a snowy wonderland and a cozy fire. You did say you brought the watches with you, right?"

She was still staring at him, probably wondering if he'd suffered a concussion in the last fifteen minutes.

"Yes. I have watches. But you..." Her eyes narrowed on him. "Max, are you agreeing to do the commercial for Isaac?"

"No." Some of the hope dashed from her expression, but he restored it with his next words. "I'm agreeing to do the commercial for *you*."

Eight

One minute he was making an offer he never saw coming, and the next he was covered in wet, giggling woman.

Kendall sliced through the water and wrapped her arms around his neck, crushing his larynx and rendering him deaf in one ear when she squealed her gratitude.

"Oh my God! If this works, I'll owe you big-time!" One more tight squeeze of his neck and she released him. Her eyes danced with merriment, her rosy cheeks rosier than before. She was wrapped around him, her Lycra-covered breasts brushing his chest beneath the water, her mouth poised to be kissed.

So.

He kissed her.

His lips met hers gently, but he gave her room to push him away while allowing enough space to excuse himself if he'd been reading her wrong.

Turned out, he hadn't been reading her wrong.

She slanted her mouth over his and tightened her hold on his neck, her mouth warm and welcome, the scent of peppermint invading his senses.

The odd compliment she'd given him about how he smelled like the outdoors, as well as the furtive glances she'd been sending him when she didn't think he'd noticed, added up to one simple equation.

She wanted him.

And hell, he was all aboard that sailing ship.

She ended the kiss with a soft smooching sound but didn't let him go. His hands were wrapped around her ribs, his thumbs brushing the tails of the knot between her breasts. Still room to back off if they'd made a mistake.

"I didn't mean to do that." She lifted her eyebrows and waited for his response. If she thought he'd take her to task for the kiss, she couldn't be more wrong.

"I'm glad you did."

"Oh."

He smoothed his hands down to her waist and back up again, watching heat flare in the depths of her dark eyes. "Do it again. See if it's any better the second time around."

His lips brushed hers as he spoke and again, she didn't back off. Instead, she obeyed his command—more a plea at this point—and smothered him with another kiss.

The woman could *kiss*. Her mouth moved on his with confidence and hunger, yet there was a timidity about the way she held her body in check. Even though his hands were on her and her breasts occasionally touched his chest beneath the water, she wasn't rubbing on him the way he'd like. The way she'd like, too, if she gave in and tried it.

As he'd reminded himself earlier, he wasn't a saint. A hot-and-heavy hookup was fine with him. One with a woman who lived on the other side of the country was even better. Relationships ate into the peace and privacy he'd worked so hard to attain.

The woman in his hot tub currently tangling her tongue with his ticked the right boxes, but Kendall was a messy option. She was Isaac's. Not his girlfriend, but she worked with him. An entanglement between Kendall and Max could end detrimental. Especially now that he'd agreed to pretend to be his brother in the commercial.

She pulled away from his mouth, her eyes shut as she hummed. "You're right. Definitely better the second time around."

He blew out a laugh.

She opened her eyes. There was nothing in those dark depths but hope now. None of the despair or defeat he'd spotted before. Why did scaring off her demons make him feel so good?

She pushed off his shoulders and swam to the other side of the hot tub. Max, erection standing on end, fought to stay seated rather than follow and tear her bikini top off with his teeth.

"So, what do I do now?"

Mind still stuck on having sex with her, he had plenty of suggestions, and a few that would get him slapped.

"Film the commercial on my iPhone?" she asked, and then he realized they weren't agonizing over the same topic. "Convince Citizen to produce an edgy, selfie-style commercial?" A dent appeared between her eyebrows, hinting her brain was whirring away. Meanwhile, his brain was running as sluggishly as if he'd downed several shots of tequila on an empty stomach.

"Hell no," he growled. "No selfie anything."

Her smile spread into a grin. "You seem the sort to hate selfies."

"Don't get me started." He grumbled the low warning. She laughed at his faux cynicism, which eased some of the sexual tension between them. "I have film equipment. Top of the line."

"Really?" She pulled her chin back and frowned, as if she was sliding together the final pieces of the Max Dunn puzzle. "Why does the man who walked away from Hollywood, and swore never to return, own film equipment?"

Talk about a question he didn't want to answer. He wasn't the least bit shy or awkward any longer, but he found himself feeling a strange cocktail of both. The endeavor he was working on was private, and nothing he'd shared with anyone. The subjects of his project couldn't talk. That was most of their appeal.

Kendall cocked her head in curiosity, waiting for

his answer. He figured a blow-off wouldn't work, not that he could think of a plausible lie after she'd turned his brain into Silly Putty.

"I'm filming a documentary." He tensed, waiting for her reaction, which was one part what he'd expected and one part what he hadn't. The part he'd expected was the look of surprise on her pretty face. The part he didn't was her smile of interest.

"Tell me about it."

Unused to discussing his passion, he shifted uncomfortably before remembering he was a grown-ass man. He was also still part Danny Brooks, and Max knew the world would be as skeptical of him attempting something deep and serious as they were of Jim Carrey when he veered from his comedic roots to make *The Truman Show*.

"It's a nature documentary. I'm filming wildlife on my property. Learning about them and their life cycles. It's a commentary on how we are surrounded by beauty, but rarely open our eyes to notice it. Notice it, and stop tearing down forests to build apartment complexes."

Well, that was honest. He could have just stopped at "it's a nature documentary."

"Wow." She appeared and sounded awed, which he didn't quite know what to do with. "Who are you selling it to?"

"No one yet."

She fluttered her lashes a few times like she was processing information at a rapid pace. "I'm trying really hard not to slip into agent mode and give you a list of tasks to ensure we sell this documentary to the highest bidder."

"We?"

She looked down, and then peeked up at him through her lashes. "Slip of the tongue."

"We did that already." There it came again, the sexual tension that rippled along the surface of the water and increased his body temperature significantly. "Care to do it again?"

"And miss the opportunity to talk you into signing with me, letting me see footage and pitching it to a studio as soon as the Wi-Fi is up and running?" Her smile was adorably self-effacing. "I'd much rather kiss you."

Those words were the gunshot signaling the beginning of a race. He was off the bench and reaching through the velvet water to scoop her against him a second later. She responded the way he wanted, moaning into his mouth before he slipped his tongue against hers. Her fingernails dug into his shoulders as he moved to a seat and gathered her ass in his hands. She settled over his erection, which hadn't gone anywhere, setting him aflame with her skillful mouth. He speared his fingers into her hair, pulled into a sloppy knot at the top of her head, and tugged her mouth hard against his.

When she sank her hands below the water to touch his stomach, he had to pull away to suck in a breath.

"Is this okay?" she asked, raking her fingers down his abs.

"Yes. Hell yes. More than okay. Don't stop."

She tipped her head back to laugh at his border-line pleading, and he took advantage of her position to lick a trail from her throat to her ear. Her smile faded into a low hum he felt against his lips.

The water was silky between them but he wanted to feel how silky she was without the bikini. He wanted her naked. And so he told her, "I want you naked, California. Get your ass inside."

He punctuated his request with a squeeze to one butt cheek he couldn't wait to take a bite of once they were out of this hot tub.

She was watching him with what might be uncertainty, which prompted him to slow down and let his brain have a say in this conversation.

"Did you have something else in mind?"

"I— No, I mean yes. I mean, no. I want that, too. But I didn't think you'd want to… with me."

"You kidding me?" he asked through a low laugh, because how could she be serious?

"I find you incredibly attractive, Max. It's been a while since I've been um, delighted in the bedroom, so to speak."

"Delighted?" His voice was laced with humor. She caught the nuance and grinned.

"You know what I mean!" She half shoved, half splashed his shoulder.

"I find you extremely attractive. And if you're afraid I won't delight you in the bedroom, I beg of you, give me a chance to prove you wrong."

"Just one chance?" Her fingers played in the longer, damp strands of his hair.

"Let's start with one." He leaned forward and she melted against him. The move held the heat and sensuality of a moment ago, but was more curious and explorative this time around. Either way—slow or fast—was fine with him.

He slipped her off his lap and stood. "You first. I'll close up the tub."

"Okay." She sounded breathless and looked like she was about to serve herself up to him on a platter. She had a gorgeous body from what he'd seen. Smallish breasts, thick hips, slim waist. Her hair was falling thanks to him sliding his fingers into it. He couldn't wait to see those caramel-colored locks unleashed on his pillow.

"My room," he instructed when she grabbed her towel and ran to the back door. "You can hang your suit and towel in the shower."

"You mean *my* room?" she asked with a cheeky smile. He returned it, feeling a strange sensation he hadn't felt in a long, long while. Like running into an old friend unexpectedly and welcoming them with open arms.

If he wasn't mistaken, that old friend was Happiness.

Nine

Max had come upstairs to find her rinsing off in his shower. He'd joined her and soon they were continuing what they'd started in the hot tub. She preferred the shower, though, since they were both naked. She'd soaped him up, weighing his sizable cock in her palm as he'd slipped fingers between her folds.

By the time he'd moaned her name into her mouth, she was already disintegrating beneath his touch.

Now, one orgasm later, she was laid across his bed, her hair slightly wet from shower spray, her eyes heavy and her body warm and relaxed.

"Don't you fall asleep on me." He rubbed the towel over his too-long hair and came to her in long-legged steps.

"It's not my fault you turned me into a puddle."

"We're not done yet."

She found the bossy version of him more welcome when he was about to have sex with her. He started by kissing her mouth, which he was very good at, and then moved to her earlobes and nibbled his way down her neck. He weaved his fingers with hers and pressed her palm flat against the bed. He repeated the motion with her other hand, settling it down with a soft *whump* as it hit the blankets. A tiny gasp of surprise escaped her throat.

"How long since you've been *delighted*, Kendall?"

"An eternity," she whispered.

"Me, too." He gave her a fast kiss and let his weight and heat settle over her body, smashing her into the mattress in an entirely pleasant way. "Do I need a condom, or are you protected?"

"From having babies with you, you mean?"

"That's what I mean." An almost gooey, definitely warm expression flitted across his face. Then she blinked and whatever she thought she saw was gone.

"My birth control is intact. Feel free to go bareback."

"Bareback." He growled before kissing her hard, his tongue plundering her mouth while she fought to keep pace. Then his tongue was circling her nipple. He moved to the other breast as she squirmed beneath him, pushing against his hands shackling her. He tightened his hold and a zing of pleasure shot up and down her body as another orgasm built low in her belly.

"Max."

"Right here, beautiful." He was over her now, regarding her with those hypnotizing blue eyes. "Ready?"

Her *yes* was a barely audible breath.

He sank in gently, first slipping the tip of his penis between her folds, then tilting and thrusting forward until he hit gold.

She shouted his name this time, which made him grin. "Men. So cocky."

"Say that word again," he dared. She became suddenly shy and shook her head. "Okay, fine. But I'm replaying it in my head the entire time we do this. You're going to come again, and then I'll try for a third time for you. No promises, though. You're hotter than hell and I'm already half gone."

She processed each part of his speech slowly, absorbing how he wanted to give her two—maybe three—orgasms. And how he might not last long thanks to how hot he found her. She was beyond flattered.

A few strokes later she came again. He loosened his hold on her hands, which was just as well since she couldn't move. Mouth set to her breast again, he continued plunging deep, each sensual slide making her ache for more. She was almost too tired to go again, but he was commanding in this way as well, and his body wouldn't let hers deny its most primal urges.

She clutched, her inner muscles clamping onto his cock, and came. He followed, spilling inside her as he practically shouted in her ear. His body tensed, the muscles in his back and shoulders as solid as steel. She stroked his smooth back, enjoying the feeling of him moving within her, the weight of his body against hers, his heat keeping her from being cold. Then he relaxed, a long sigh curling from his lungs to wrap around her throat, where he'd set his mouth.

She reached up and touched his hair, playing with the soft strands as he relaxed further. Her eyes closed, she enjoyed the moment here with her snowed-in mountain man who'd agreed to do a commercial not for his brother, but for *her*.

Because as much as Max pretended not to care about anyone, he did care.

She squeezed him against her and kissed his cheek once, twice. He twisted his neck and gave her his mouth and she kissed him there for a long, long while.

When he pulled away, again she sensed something deeper and untraveled in his eyes, which scared her a little. It was unfamiliar ground, a man caring about her. The men she'd dated seemed to have a backup plan in mind. If things didn't work out with her, they'd known where to go next.

She'd never planned ahead. She stayed in the moment. Which was probably the smartest move with Max.

He had an end date. As soon as the snow melted and the commercial footage was filmed, she'd fly back in California. She wasn't leaving LA. He wasn't going to move away from the town named after him. They were well and truly temporary. But after that bout of fantastic sex, she couldn't make herself regret kissing him.

"Well?" He studied her in the moonlight-streaked bedroom. Worrying he'd seen her thoughts play across her face, she opted to lighten the moment.

"Delightful," she said.

His beautiful smile bloomed, widening until his throat moved with a deep, luscious laugh. It might have been the most lovely sound she'd ever heard. She wanted to bottle it and open the top whenever she felt down.

"I completely agree." He stood from the bed and grabbed her hand. "One more shower."

"Another?" she groaned, dragging her feet to the bathroom as best as she could on spent legs. He spun the knob and stepped into the water, pulling her in with him.

Yes, she decided, while she was in Dunn she would take this thing with Max one day at a time. Or more accurately, since her time here was limited, one *hour* at a time.

Max's eyes popped open just before 5:00 a.m. like they did every other morning. Unlike every other morning, he wasn't already throwing off the blankets and beelining for the coffeepot. Reason being, there was a woman lying on his chest.

A delicate, luminescent, stunning creature…who snored. Really, it sounded like a helicopter was flying over his house.

She sucked in a sound like a honk and then jerked

awake, her eyes blinking slowly around the room before they landed on his face.

Then her smile went wonky and her eyes lowered to half-mast. Her hand swept over his nipples and down his stomach before traveling up again. His cock stirred to life in an instant.

"Was I snoring?" she asked with a frown.

"Like an industrial-sized vacuum."

She shoved his chest, appearing offended before burying her face in her hands. "I hate cold weather! This doesn't happen at home, I swear."

"Don't sweat it," he told her, meaning it. "I sleep deep. I only noticed after I woke up. You want coffee?"

"It's pitch-black outside. What time is it?"

He told her and she nearly passed out from shock. "I cannot get out of bed at five in the morning."

"You don't have to get out of bed." He rolled her onto her back and kissed her. She made a sleepy noise as he moved down her body, until he reached her thighs. Then her breaths went high and tight, and her fingers nested in his hair. "You steer, I'll operate the gas pedal."

She laughed, sounding tired. She wouldn't stay that way if he had anything to say about it.

He spread her legs and kissed her inner thighs. Slowly, tickling her skin with his bearded chin before breathing over her center and kissing her other thigh. He'd been content to continue the leisurely pace, but Kendall decided she was done waiting. Hands on his ears, she steered him where she wanted him to go.

He allowed her the move, but took over when his mouth hit heaven.

He knew exactly what to do down here.

Listening carefully as he tried a few different tricks, he quickly learned what she liked. Firm pressure with his tongue, his hands holding her legs open and his fingertips gripping her flesh.

She twisted her fingers in his hair and arched her back. Pushed against his face and retreated with a high cry. He didn't let up for a second. Not even when an orgasm rocked her and her thighs slammed over his ears. Fine by him, he didn't mind being trapped. But when he renewed his efforts, she begged him to stop.

"I can't..." Her hair was a tangled mess on his pillow. Her eyes heavy from pleasure as much as sleep. Then she grinned down at him. Perfect. "Your turn."

Okay, *now* it was perfect.

He intended to further stretch out their pleasure, but she accepted his length with a sigh of gratitude that made it harder for him to hold back. She undulated beneath him, pushing down when he thrust up, saying his name, *pleading* his name. Then she reversed their positions, her on top, her breasts pushed together, her hands resting on his chest. Her forehead crinkled into pain-pleasure folds as she rode him.

It was dirty and fantastic and yeah, perfect.

When they'd both worn each other out, they collapsed in a tangled heap on his twisted sheets.

Not long after, her eyelids drooped again. "It's

too early for coffee," she murmured as she rolled to one side. "But not for that."

"It's never too early for that," he said but she was already asleep, the start of a snore brewing in the back of her throat.

"I'm not done with you yet, California." She wasn't a woman he could sleep with once and forget about. Hell, he was already behaving out of character and she'd been here, what? Two days. He'd agreed to shoot a commercial. Him. Max Dunn, who hated commercials. And he'd told her—an agent—about his documentary, which he'd refuse to sell to the highest bidder when that would be her natural inclination. Not that he wouldn't sell... He'd simply insist on full creative control.

He wasn't sure what to make of his thoughts. It was like Kendall had brought a former version of him out of hiding. The hopeful and light version, rather than the jaded and washed up one.

He covered her with the blankets and pulled on his winter wardrobe of jeans and layered, warm shirts. Then he shut the door on his bedroom and headed downstairs to make some coffee.

An hour later, he was staring at the flames in the fireplace, his own eyes growing heavy. He was happy. Relaxed. For the first time in years, he was questioning his version of utopia. He'd convinced himself existing here, alone, was the best place for him. And after the split with Bunny, it became clear he should never attempt to bring a woman into his space again.

But Kendall was here. In his space. And he felt better than he had in years. Interesting.

He stood to refill his coffee mug, watching as more snow fell on the trees outside his window.

She was too Hollywood for him. Too stubborn a match for his own stubborn attitude. *And* she snored.

She was also living with him short-term without any preconceived notions or worries. Maybe that was why her presence—and her snoring—wasn't a turnoff.

Or maybe it was simply the way she made him want to protect her. To bolster her, to be there for her in case she fell. Or in case she nearly froze to death walking from her car to his house during a blizzard.

"Have one of those for me?" he heard behind him. Kendall, hair pulled into a ponytail, wore a long T-shirt and leggings, and a pair of his bulky socks. She sashayed into the kitchen, looking sexier than she had a right to.

"Yeah. Here." He handed over his coffee mug. Just like he'd handed over his bed, and his scruples when it came to throwing himself to the Hollywood sharks again.

But he'd done that for her, a decision that came with its own issues, which he chose to ignore for now.

"Thanks." She accepted the mug and pushed to her tiptoes to lay a soft kiss on the center of his mouth. Then her eyes widened with excitement. "Do you think the Wi-Fi is working?"

By the time she bounced upstairs, and down again with her laptop, he reminded himself that lending his bed or his acting skills to her was one thing. Handing over more of himself was out of the question. For a lot of reasons, the main one being the way commitment changed some people. They could go from soft and sweet and loving to greedy and self-consumed... or maybe that had just been Bunny.

"Still down! How do you get anything done here?" Kendall asked.

"I don't." He embraced her and pressed his lips to the top of her head while she went on about how modern life and wildlife had a hard time coexisting.

She didn't seem to be pulling a bait and switch the way his ex had. Kendall was different from Bunny in every way—at her very core. Kendall was striving to go somewhere he'd gone a long time ago. To the summit of Mount Success. He'd been there, done that, had his face on the T-shirt.

If he'd learned anything from his previous marriage, it was that two people with radically different goals, much like modern life and wildlife, *couldn't* coexist.

The sex was fun. Kendall was fun. But when the time came for her to go back to LA, he'd have no problem with her leaving.

He'd drive her to the airport himself.

Ten

"Thank you," Kendall said before ending the call to the mechanic.

"Well?" Max strode into the room, looking delicious and smelling better.

"He said they can get the car back to one hundred percent, no problem. They have to order a part. It could take three days or two weeks. Think you'd have better luck talking to them since you're a man?"

"Who'd you talk to?"

"Hank, I think?"

He pressed a kiss to her forehead. "He wouldn't lie to you, California. You ready to go?"

They were going into town today. Max was confident his truck would navigate the snow and the now-salted roads thanks to his buddy, Luca, who'd even cleared the parking pad in front of Max's garage.

She'd emailed Citizen the moment the Wi-Fi came on yesterday evening. She'd explained how she and "Isaac" were trapped in a snowy mountain town, luckily with high-end film equipment. She'd attached a few photos of Max's cabin's interior to show them how beautiful it was. She didn't share more details than necessary and nearly chewed her nails to the quick waiting for them to respond. She'd won over Max. Could she win over Citizen?

This afternoon she received an email from them and shrieked with delight. They'd had a marketing meeting first thing this morning and everyone liked the locale better than the original idea of a studio shoot. They'd also run into issues with the production company they'd hired and were looking to replace them. There was only one problem: They couldn't very well fly out the model they'd screen-tested for the shoot thanks to the blizzard.

Kendall replied that she had acting experience and was more than willing to step into the role for the sake of the brand and Isaac's contract. She assured them she could handle it, and attached a few selfies.

For two hours, she'd panicked over that email. First off, she was not a model. Being Miss North Carolina in a pageant back home wasn't the same as acting in commercials. She also worried that appearing in an ad with Isaac would lead to awkward negotiations as his agent in the future. Would other sponsors take her seriously if they believed she and Isaac were *together*?

She eventually dismissed the worry. She'd seen enough ads with enough hot guys in them to know no one paid attention to the women in those ads. All eyes would be on Max, or, as they'd let the public believe, Isaac.

Citizen loved the idea of her being in the ad, and had sent a very, very detailed list of footage and wardrobe requirements, if that wasn't a problem. She assured them it was no problem at all, and that she and her client could make it into town where there were all manner of shops and stores to fill their needs.

"I'm ready," she answered, slipping on a pair of high heels.

"We're going to buy you some boots today, too. *Real* boots."

Dunn was rural but the town, much like Max's cabin, was upscale. Tall house-like buildings lined the sidewalks. Jagged snowcapped mountain ranges interspersed with pine trees made up the picturesque background.

Max maneuvered around frozen piles of snow, mountains in their own way, and parked in an open spot on the somewhat-deserted street. She was surprised to find locals bustling around, as if they weren't in the middle of a blizzard.

"You all seem used to the weather."

"Not much keeps us indoors. We moved to Million Dollar Mountain to experience nature. Plus," he said, climbing out of the truck, "we have everything we need right here."

She looked around the immediate area and saw he was right. She spotted a coffee shop, bookstore—those were rare—and a shoe store. A supermarket took up most of the street on the other side, and the shop in front of where Max parked, sold suits and ties.

He opened her door and looked down at her shoes, shaking his head. "Boots first." Then he turned and gave her his back. "Hop on."

"Seriously?"

He was serious and communicated that by looking over his shoulder, raising one dark eyebrow, and saying, "California."

She swung her legs out, gripped his shoulders and did as instructed, hopping onto his back. He held her thighs in his big palms, kicked his truck door closed and maneuvered her around the piles of snow before settling her onto the sidewalk.

"It'll be interesting to see you spiffed up again, Max Dunn. I've grown accustomed to your mountain man vibe."

"Guessing Citizen doesn't want a mountain man."

No, but I do, she thought. She'd been enjoying snowy days working at his house, and spending her evenings with him. More explicitly: her evenings in his bed.

They walked three doors down to the shoe store, where she was impressed to find a wide selection.

She touched the toe of a pair of Jimmy Choos, but he grasped her hand and dragged her two aisles over.

"Boots," he reminded her, pointing at the less desirable footwear.

Thirty minutes and two pairs of shoes later—because come on, who could pass up bubble-gum pink Jimmy Choos?—Max stored her purchases in the back seat of his Dodge Ram and they went suit shopping.

"What did Citizen say they wanted?" he asked as a man with a measuring tape dangling around his neck entered the shopping area.

"Charcoal gray, as dark as you can find."

"Max!" the man greeted, extending a hand.

Max shook it, his smile warmer than she would have expected. "Hey, Darnell. This is Kendall Squire. She can tell you what I need. I sure as hell can't."

First Luca, then Hank at the garage, and now Darnell. Her reclusive mountain man seemed to have an awful lot of friends.

"Sounds like we're in this together, Kendall." Darnell laughed as he looped his arm in hers and led her to a rack of jackets. "What do you like?"

Max was cooperative, which also surprised her. He tried on jackets and pants, and a few different ties. When she commented on his compliance, he sent her a look that was both hungry and teasing, which tempted her to drag him into the nearest dressing room and ravish him.

Unfortunately, Darnell was very attentive. She insisted on paying and charging Citizen, but Max refused. After their argument prompted an interruption from Darnell, she let Max do as he pleased. Something else she was coming to terms with about him—he did what he wanted. So did she, but he took stubbornness to an advanced level.

Darnell thanked them for their business and Max told him to say hello to Lisa. "His wife," Max explained as he opened the door for Kendall.

"See?" She hugged his arm with both of hers. "That wasn't so bad. I bet you thought—"

"Max!"

Kendall stopped short and came face-to-face with a smiling, petite blonde with fantastic cheekbones and captivating blue eyes. Those blue eyes studied Kendall carefully, assessing, before she addressed Max again.

"What made you fight the snow and ice to shop at Stockwood's?" She nodded at the shop he and Kendall had just exited and then gave Max an exaggerated wink. "Is there a big fancy dinner you needed a suit for, or something?"

Whatever that meant. The other woman laughed but Max remained rigid. When it was apparent he wasn't going to introduce her, Kendall offered a hand and gave the other woman her name.

"Bunny Chambers." The blonde captured Kendall's hand with her gloved one and pumped twice. She had a firm grip for her slim frame—which Kendall could tell was slim even under a puffy, waist-length coat. "Max and I used to be married."

"O-oh," Kendall stammered, unable to hide her

surprise. She knew he'd been married a few years back, but her research hadn't uncovered photos of Mrs. Dunn. Or, well, Ms. Chambers, as it were.

"You're overdue for a haircut," Bunny informed Max. Accurately. "I'm a stylist," she told Kendall. "And the mayor's wife. He's running for reelection soon." She turned to Max again. "Have you had second thoughts about asking Isaac for a reference for me?" Rather than wait for his answer, which judging by his silence he wasn't about to offer, Bunny spoke to Kendall again. "I cut hair, but I've always wanted to be an actress. If Max here would hook me up with a call from the Coast, I could be well on my way." She speared Max with a glare that hardened her pretty features. "What do you do, Kendall?"

"I'm a—"

"She's a stylist, too. Was driving through Dunn when she stuck her car in the snow. I'm showing her around," Max interrupted.

A flare of what might have been jealousy sparked in the other woman's eyes before she seemed to remember her manners. She offered a stiff smile. "How fun. Well, I should be going. Late for work." She waved and turned on one boot heel before disappearing in to the salon a few doors down.

"I'm a stylist?"

"You're going to be when you trim my hair," he informed her. Then he turned and offered her his back. "On."

"Before I ride you to your truck, I need to pop

into the supermarket and pick up a few things for the shoot."

He straightened. "Like what?"

"Like a mister so we can spray ourselves with water. Don't you want to look fresh?"

"What am I, a bed of lettuce?" he grumbled, but to her he didn't sound all that upset. More like he thought he should be and was playing his part.

"Speaking of which, how about lunch? What's good?"

"Rocky's is the best, but he's closed during the blizzard. The café has sandwiches, though. If you're tired of my home cooking."

"Your home cooking is delicious, but a little light on the green stuff." She grasped his hand and squeezed. "Take me to lunch, Mountain Man. Let's see if we can find a salad in this town."

Not only did they find a salad, but a California Cobb salad. No avocado, though, thanks to the blizzard keeping deliveries out of town. Kendall was starting to miss home. Thankfully she found a tub of prepared guacamole, and while it wasn't fresh avocado, it was better than nothing. After the market, she stopped by a drugstore to buy a pair of haircutting scissors.

Back home, Max lit a fire. She carried her shopping bag upstairs, traded the high-heeled shoes she was wearing for a pair of his thick socks, and padded downstairs to find him putting away their groceries.

She leaned on the counter and watched him move around the kitchen. She imagined another woman here with him. A slim blonde with hard, but pretty features who wanted to be an actress. It was difficult to picture them married. Had he loved her? Had he carried her upstairs to make love to her or kissed her in the hot tub? He would have had to, wouldn't he?

"Why did you tell Bunny I was a stylist?"

"Because if you would have told her you're a talent agent she'd never leave me alone." He set the kettle on the burner and turned it on High. Then he leaned against the counter and folded his arms over his chest. "The day you showed up and knocked on my door, Bunny was here earlier, pacing back and forth in my cabin, telling me how she needed her big break before Greg Chambers was reelected mayor. She doesn't want to be stuck in this town. She dreams of a life in Hollywood."

Kendall blinked. That made Bunny and Max a definite mismatch.

"She wasn't always like that. She told me when we were first married she wanted a simple life and a family. Three months later, she changed her mind. After two tumultuous years of marriage, we were divorced. That was three years ago. She's over me, happily married—at least I think they're happy—but she never lost her lust for making it big."

"She seemed…" Hard. Jealous. Shrewd. "Nice."

A half smile slipped onto his face. "Sweet of you to say, California, but one thing Bunny never was, was nice. Tea?"

"Sure."

He pulled two mugs from the cabinet and said no

more about his ex-wife. Meanwhile, Kendall's mind was spinning with thoughts. About the commercial. About Bunny. About Max.

"Does she bring that up often?" Kendall asked conversationally. "The acting thing?"

"Only every chance she gets. When she heard *Brooks Knows Best* was getting the band back together, she ran over here asking me if I was going to participate. When I told her no, she tried to talk me into it."

"Is she any good?" Realizing that sounded like she was asking about sex, Kendall rephrased. "Is she a good actress?"

"No." A twinkle lit his eyes when he added, "On both counts."

Eleven

Kendall chewed on her lip and watched him carefully. Too carefully. He could hear her wheels grinding. Over what, he had no clue. He handed over her tea and took a seat on the sofa, making room for her when she practically sat on top of him.

He liked her close, there was no denying it. But alarm bells went off inside him when he noticed her gaze was unfocused on the fire. A sure sign her brain was turning over idea after idea—and so far most of them he hadn't liked.

"I have an idea," she declared, proving him right.

"Unless it involves us naked, the answer is no." He smiled when she leaned in and kissed him. He could kiss her all damn day. She was receptive and sexy, fun to hang out with even when complaining about the lack of fresh avocados, but she was more fun to kiss.

She pulled away, licking her lips and touching his beard. "It so happens I'm a beauty school dropout. I can cut hair. So in a way you told Bunny the truth."

"Oh, good, I'll be able to sleep soundly now," he said, deadpan.

"What if I found her a part on *Brooks Knows Best*?"

He stiffened.

"Hear me out. If she's good enough for a small part, you won't have to worry about her harassing you any longer."

"Yeah, but you will. She'll be your client. Sure you want to chum those waters?" Kendall was such a curious creature to him. He couldn't figure out if she was trying to legitimately help everyone, or if trying to help others was how she disguised helping herself.

"I admit, being down to my last client makes me a little desperate. Unless *you* want to sign with me. Maybe after this watch commercial, you can shoot a cologne ad."

The prospect shot more rigidity into his spine. Moving away from her, he picked up his mug and rested his elbows on his knees.

"Explain to me why doing what you were very good at doing for years is so abhorrent to you now."

"Because I've seen behind the curtain." He stood and waved his fingers like casting a spell. "I've seen the man working the controls, and he's more devious than anyone knows. Even you, I suspect."

"Well, you're wrong," she said with not much confidence.

"You're new at this, California. You might have lived in LA doing odd jobs, but you haven't been in the industry long. When talent is being swapped for dollars, it's cheapened."

"I beg your pardon." She was on her feet now, too. "I make people's dreams come true."

"Keep telling yourself that."

Her mouth dropped open, fire lighting her dark eyes. He liked seeing that fire, but not because he'd pissed her off. He'd overstepped. Let the run-in with his ex-wife become personal.

Kendall was halfway up the stairs when he walked to the base and rested his hand on the bannister. He didn't want to fight with her, especially over Bunny, or Hollywood—two things he no longer loved.

"She didn't want to have a family. That's why we split." He was supposed to say he was sorry, but ended up confessing that whopper.

Kendall, one foot frozen in midair, spun and walked down a step toward him. Her expression had gone from fiery hurt to deep concern.

"I know it's a blessing now," he continued. "God knows we'd have ended up divorced no matter what, and I would never want to put a kid through that. She started talking about Hollywood and needing to keep her options open, and I resented her for it. She changed the rules." He shrugged. Out of things to say on the topic.

As he expected, Kendall offered a heartfelt "I'm

sorry" but he didn't expect what came next. "Can I see some of what you've filmed?"

She confused him for a second before he realized she meant his wildlife documentary. "It's not a state secret."

"You seem awfully protective of it."

"Haven't you learned yet—" he climbed to the middle of the staircase to meet her "—I'm the protective sort?"

Head tipped, her lips parted softly. Then they snapped shut and she walked up a few steps, putting distance between them. "I can protect myself. I'm making dinner tonight, by the way. Don't touch my scallops."

She finished her trek to his bedroom and softly closed the door. He wondered if "scallops" was a double entendre for something kinky, but then he figured, probably not.

Her mug of untouched tea sat on the coffee table, in front of a crackling fire next to the sofa where they had just been sitting with their hips touching. He wished they were still sitting there.

He liked her too much to argue and then end in separate rooms. Besides, she was going to be holding a pair of sharp scissors close to his face soon. Best to stay on her good side. Though he trusted her with a sharp object near him more than his ex-wife.

He wasn't sure what prompted him to share the real reason for his and Bunny's split. Temporary insanity, perhaps. Or maybe Kendall had a way of softening him up and bending him to her will. If so, he'd better get a hold of himself before he turned into a damn songbird.

Which reminded him, he still needed to find and film an evening grosbeak before winter was over. They'd been hard to spot this season, despite their vibrant yellow coloring and bold black-and-white wings. He was cataloging every season here in Virginia for his doc, and it wouldn't be complete without the grosbeak.

Upstairs, he collected his camera equipment, pausing at his bedroom door and debating whether to tell Kendall he was leaving. He heard the telltale clacking of keyboard keys and opted to leave her to her work.

Which, he supposed, was what he was to her now, as well. Another client, another paycheck. Onward, onward to commercial success.

Kendall was chopping vegetables for a salad when Max came in through the front door. She paused, the knife hovering over the strip of red bell pepper she was about to chop into neat squares. A blast of relief hit her at the same time the outdoor wind curled around her bare arms and sent a shiver over her body. She'd been overly warm moving around the kitchen and had shed her sweater in favor of the T-shirt underneath.

She'd assumed he was angry with her for walking away from him, which only seemed fair as she was just as angry with herself. What she should have done when he'd hovered over her was grab a fistful of his shirt and tug his lips to hers. Then she could have kissed him until they ended up naked and having sex on the stairs.

She'd been sensitive earlier after his assessment of who she was and what she was doing in her career. Silly, really. Why did what he thought matter to her? Soon she'd be flying home and she'd probably never see him again, anyway. But he hadn't been the only one who'd spoken out of turn. She'd started it.

"Hi." She set the knife down. "I was wondering where you were."

He held up a fancy video camera with one gloved hand. He was dressed in a heavier coat than he'd been wearing earlier, this one with a fur-lined hood. His nose and his cheeks above his dark beard were red from the cold. Snow was melting on his hair and his eyelashes. "Had to shoot some footage today."

"I'd like to see it." She held up her hands in mock surrender. "Not because I'm going to talk you into sending it off to a film studio."

He set down his camera and shed his coat. She came out from behind the counter and rubbed her hands together. She owed him an apology, so she might as well get it over with.

"I'm ambitious," she started.

"You don't say."

"Don't be smart." But a smile sneaked onto her lips at his tone. He was funny when he tried to be, and right now, he was trying. "I shouldn't have mentioned you signing with me. I won't do it again. I haven't been very respectful of your boundaries. That changes tonight."

Her piece said, she nodded and returned to chopping pepper squares for the salad. A moment later, his heat blanketed her back, contrasting the feel of his cold nose when he kissed her cheek. She didn't mean to lean into him, but she did.

"I'm sorry I talked to you like you were young and inexperienced." His hands linked around her waist, he tugged her bottom against his firm hips. "You're on a different speed from me and I'm not used to it."

"You mean because I work for a living and you're a retired bird-watcher?"

He spun her so she was facing him, a much better view for her. Those long dark lashes, blue eyes gazing into her like he was imagining her without her clothes. "Think you're cute?"

She grinned, easily detecting the playfulness in his gruff tone. "Uh-huh. I do."

"You're right." He bent and cupped her ass in his hands and hoisted her up, then carried her to one countertop and then the other before finding them both filled with ingredients for their dinner. "Damn, woman, haven't you heard of cleaning as you go?"

"I'm so sorry, Mary Poppins. I'm not up to speed on your housekeeping rules."

The jab did what she expected, propelling him into action. He moved from the kitchen to the couch, laying her onto her back and reaching for the button of her jeans.

"I'm in the middle of cooking dinner."

"It's going to have to wait."

"Is that so?" she asked as he tugged her pants halfway off her legs.

"That's so. I'm cold. I'm tired. Make-up sex is the only thing on the menu." He maneuvered his hand beneath her T-shirt. She expected his hands to be cold, but they were warm from the gloves he'd been wearing. Or maybe from his own elevated core temperature.

His next kiss turned her inside out. Then her shirt was gone, her pants on the floor. It'd been a long, long time since she'd had make-up sex. She hadn't had a relationship with a guy who was worth arguing with for as long as she could remember. She didn't realize she'd missed it—the interacting, even the disagreeing. Especially the making-up part.

Max was very, very good at the making-up part.

Twelve

The man could eat.

Kendall sliced a scallop in half and tenderly took the bite onto her tongue. Meanwhile, Max ate two at a time.

She could tell he enjoyed dinner, even if he didn't savor it. Cooking for him made her feel light and happy, and she imagined cooking for him in warmer weather, a cheery strand of lights strung over an outdoor dinner table. Outside, the snow sat fat and untouched on the patio railing and on the steps leading to what she guessed was a yard. Right now, there was nothing but snow, snow and more snow.

"It's official." He sat back and pulled a hand over his taut middle. "You can't leave if you're going to continue to cook like this. Where'd you learn how?"

"Necessity. I like good food and the restaurants in LA are outrageous. Not that I have to tell you. You know firsthand."

"Not so." He scooped another spoonful of French green beans onto his plate, followed by more scallops in lemon butter sauce. "Most of my meals were free in LA. I ate like a king."

"And you gave it up for this." She gestured out the window. "Isn't it hard looking out the window and seeing nothing but bleak, blue-hued cold?"

"Isn't it boring looking out your window and seeing nothing but the same weather every damn day?"

"You make a good point."

"It's more beautiful than you're giving it credit for, especially when the snow melts and the wildflowers bloom on the mountainside."

How did he do that? Go from gruff to almost poetic when talking about where he lived.

"You don't believe me," he stated.

"I do. I'm just not used to it."

"Honest truth?" he asked around his next bite. She nodded. He finished chewing and palmed a glass of white wine—one she'd chosen by price that ended up tasting pretty good. "It took me a long time to adjust to this pace, too."

"Well, since we're spilling our secrets," she teased with a wink, "I was a hostess at a five-star restaurant when I first moved to LA. The head chef took a liking to me and taught me how to make a few dishes." She liked sharing with him. She hadn't had anyone interested enough in the details of her life to ask. She'd been the one trotting out her résumé to anyone who would listen—trying to impress them or persuade them into employing her. Even under Lou's employ, she'd felt it necessary to remind him of her value.

"He probably wanted more than to teach you how to cook, California."

"*She* admired my moxie." Kendall lifted her chin, smiling when a dash of color took Max's cheeks. "Sometimes you're stuck in the Stone Age, Dunn."

"Yeah, I've been told that. Pardon my assumption. It's just you—" He shook his head, eyes on his dinner plate as he moved his green beans around. "You're captivating, Kendall. I don't know how someone in LA hasn't talked you into marrying him yet."

"Maybe the men I've dated are as commitment-phobic as you are." She'd always thought of herself as marriage-worthy, but the men she'd dated had been less inclined to permanence.

"I thought we were telling the truth." He abandoned his fork, giving up on the green beans, and reclaiming his wineglass.

"I told you the truth. The men I've dated in the past had no inclination to settle anywhere."

"Actors?"

"Never. One producer, but I didn't find out what he did for a living until we were in the middle of our first date. You're my first actor, Max."

"I'm honored. Can you tell if I'm faking or not?"

She laughed. "I can tell. Your insistence on being real and your resistance to helping me with the commercial gave you away. You're as transparent as cellophane."

"God, I hope not." He finished his wine and refilled his glass before offering her more. She accepted, first draining the scant amount in her glass.

"Bunny didn't cook?" she heard herself ask. She couldn't help inquiring about the woman who had made this unsettled man settle—at least for a few years.

"*Domestic* doesn't accurately describe my ex-wife."

"What did she mean when she brought up a special dinner when we ran into her?"

"Caught that, did you?" His tone suggested he'd hoped she'd missed that inference.

"I did. Is there a big affair happening? Some sort of fancy dinner or awards show, or—oh! Bachelor auction?"

"God no." He grimaced. "I mean, God no, not a bachelor auction. You're right on the other two counts. Sort of."

"What's the award for?"

His mouth pulled flat before he admitted, "It's for me."

Well, knock her over with a feather.

"Don't look so surprised. You know how many Fans' Choice awards I have?"

"Do you still have them?"

He narrowed his eyes. "Maybe. It's an honorary award of some kind. The townspeople like me, I guess."

"So much they named their town after you. *Humble* isn't a trait you wear well, Max."

"Someone has to be humble. Sure as hell isn't Isaac." There was no bitterness in his comment, simply observation.

"I was wondering…about your ex…"

"We're not done talking about her?"

"Nearly," she promised. "Is Bunny a stage name?"

"Nickname. Her name is Brenda. She's gone by Bunny since her dad coined it when she was a kid."

"That's sweet."

"She's from a good family."

"Like you," Kendall fished. "Isaac is a good person."

Max's nod was slow, but a nod all the same. "He is a good person."

"And you're a good person. Good people don't sprout out of the ground. You two were raised in the industry. I know of your mom and dad—the Dunns aren't as famous as you two, but they are known."

"Mom and Dad are good people. They love LA, which is honestly the only item in their con column. They host amazing parties, always have. It wasn't uncommon for famous people to be loitering on their back patio or floating in the swimming pool."

"You sound bored by it all."

"I'd take the people of Million Dollar Mountain any day." He met her eyes, something inviting and kind in their depths. "Present party excluded."

"You've already sung the praises of my stellar cooking."

"Yes, but I've yet to compliment you on how great you are in bed."

"If anyone else but you said that, Max Dunn, I'd storm from the room."

"Lucky me." He stood, crossed to where she sat at the table and offered a hand. "I promise copious compliments will follow."

She shook her head, but accepted his hand. How could one man be so irritating one minute and so irresistible the next?

"How good are you at this?" Max asked, eye level with Kendall's stomach. He didn't mind the vantage point when they were naked, but now, both dressed and her wielding a pair of shears, he was having his doubts.

"Normally, very good, but I've had a lot of caffeine this morning." She pretended to lose control of the scissors. He sent her a warning glare. She grinned.

If there was a grin that would be the death of him, it was the one on Kendall Squire's face. If the grin didn't kill him, the great sex might. But not immediately. Maybe in a good fifty, sixty years.

He blinked as a vision of them sitting side by side in a pair rocking chairs flashed through his mind. He adjusted his perch on the ledge of the bathtub, mildly alarmed by the visual. He wasn't one to picture his future with a woman. Especially a woman he could have no possible future with. He rubbed his hands

Get up to 4 FREE FABULOUS BOOKS You Love!

To thank you for being a loyal reader we'd like to send you up to 4 FREE BOOKS, absolutely free.

Just write "YES" on the Loyal Reader Voucher and we'll send you up to 4 Free Books and Free Mystery Gifts, altogether worth over $20, as a way of saying thank you for being a loyal reader.

Try **Harlequin® Desire** books featuring the worlds of the American elite with juicy plot twists, delicious sensuality and intriguing scandal.

Try **Harlequin Presents®** Larger-print books featuring the glamourous lives of royals and billionaires in a world of exotic locations, where passion knows no bounds.

Or **TRY BOTH!**

We are so glad you love the books as much as we do and can't wait to send you great new books.

So don't miss out, return your Loyal Reader Voucher Today!

Pam Powers

LOYAL READER
FREE BOOKS VOUCHER

YES! I Love Reading, please send me up to 4 FREE BOOKS and Free Mystery Gifts from the series I select.

Just write in "YES" on the dotted line below then return this card today and we'll send your free books & gifts asap!

➡ YES ⬅

Which do you prefer?

| ☐ **Harlequin Desire®** 225/326 HDL GRGA | ☐ **Harlequin Presents® Larger Print** 176/376 HDL GRGA | ☐ **BOTH** 225/326 & 176/376 HDL GRGM |

FIRST NAME   LAST NAME

ADDRESS

APT.#   CITY

STATE/PROV.   ZIP/POSTAL CODE

EMAIL ☐ Please check this box if you would like to receive newsletters and promotional emails from Harlequin Enterprises ULC and its affiliates. You can unsubscribe anytime.

HD/HP-520-LR21

HARLEQUIN® Reader Service — Here's how it works:

If offer card is missing write to: Harlequin Reader Service, P.O. Box 1341, Buffalo, NY 14240-8531 or visit www.ReaderService.com ▲

BUSINESS REPLY MAIL
FIRST-CLASS MAIL   PERMIT NO. 717   BUFFALO, NY

POSTAGE WILL BE PAID BY ADDRESSEE

HARLEQUIN READER SERVICE
PO BOX 1341
BUFFALO NY 14240-8571

NO POSTAGE
NECESSARY
IF MAILED
IN THE
UNITED STATES

on his spread knees as she maneuvered her way in between them.

"Don't be so nervous." She lifted one knee to bop his.

He was nervous, but not about the haircut. Nevertheless, he played along. "Just don't cut my ears. I have nice ears."

He does have nice ears.

Max sat in a sexy man-spread to accommodate her standing between his thighs. He'd already wet his hair and was wearing a towel around his neck, held together by one of her hair clips. She combed his long, wavy locks and snipped gingerly away at them. Each time she gathered hair between her fingers, she realized she'd forgotten how intimate an act cutting someone's hair could be. Of course, normally the person would be sitting in a salon chair and not facing her breasts. And, normally, she wasn't also sleeping with the person. In fact, she'd never trimmed anyone's hair other than her own. But Max's style was loose and forgiving, and the commercial called for his hair to look "casually tousled." Whatever that meant. She figured if she didn't overload it with product and left some of the longer waves, they'd be in the ballpark.

"That should do it." She ruffled the top of his hair and watched as it lay evenly—oops, except for that piece. *There.*

She was satisfied with her work, more satisfied

when he cupped the backs of her thighs. Warm and wide, his hands softly squeezed.

"This is the most distracting haircut I've ever had, California," he rumbled, moving his hands higher on her legs.

The shake in her body wasn't from the coffee as he'd earlier joked, but from desire shimmering over her like sun on desert sands.

"This close to your luscious body and I had to sit still. Torture." He didn't sit still now, turning her and tugging her onto his lap. She set aside her scissors and spun around to face him. The blue towel was still draped over his shoulders.

"You look like a superhero in a terry cloth cape." She laughed, expecting him to laugh with her. Instead, she was gifted with a rare peek at his acting talent.

He puffed his chest, craned one eyebrow and tipped his head. Then he stood, cradling her in his arms, and glanced up and into the distance, which was actually the corner of his bathroom.

"Now that I've saved you from the burning building, and you know my true identity, can I count on you to keep my secret?" Eyebrow still hoisted high, he glanced down at her. The walls of the bathroom fell away as she gazed into his blue eyes and clutched the corner of the towel. It wasn't hard to believe she was in the arms of a comic book hero, his real cape billowing on the air, as the sun set on a busy metropolis.

"Your secret's safe with me." She tightened her

hold. "I won't tell any of your friends in town how fun and carefree you are."

She worried he might take what she said the wrong way. Like he did whenever she entered into personal territory. He didn't.

"I'm not carefree with everyone. Just beautiful women who strand themselves in my cabin and demand I star in a commercial with them."

She was learning there was another side to Max. The side who was honest to a fault. He bent and kissed her and her toes literally curled. When he let her go, she blinked lazily up at his handsome face.

She was going to miss him when she returned to LA, no doubt about it. She shook off the unpleasant thought and changed the subject. "When's your suit ready?"

"Darnell promised tomorrow, but said he'd call if he finished alterations early."

"You'd better wash off those stray hairs." She gestured to his shoulders with her chin. "You look more like the superhero with mange than one who saved a city."

"Yes, ma'am." He kissed her, lingering over her smile for a few truncated seconds. When he set her on her feet and she left him to shower, she was smiling, too. She hadn't been far off with her observation.

To the people of Dunn, Max Dunn *was* a superhero. He was receiving an award at a fancy dinner/ awards show combo. They adored him. And, now that Kendall knew a side of Max other than the grouchy, bearded former actor who'd sent her packing, it wasn't hard to understand why.

Thirteen

"Jackpot," Max announced as he walked into his house.

Darnell had called that afternoon and told him to pick up his suit whenever he had time. He'd run into town and picked it up right away, along with a gift for Kendall. But she wasn't in her usual spot on the sofa, laptop glued to her legs. Nor was she in the kitchen cooking him a dinner that might well cause him to weep with joy.

"California?" He juggled the suit and the other garment bag while he shut the door and kicked off his boots.

"Here!" she called from the top of the stairs. "Sorry. I was snooping."

He choked on a laugh. Of course she was.

She waited for him on the second-to-last step, presumably to collect the kiss he planned on giving her. He'd gone from living by himself to "honey I'm home" in an alarmingly short amount of time.

Her standing on the second-to-last step meant he didn't have to so much as bend his neck to put his lips on hers. She kissed him back, wrapping her arms around his neck and humming her approval low in her throat.

"Best response I've had to admitting I was snooping." Her dark-with-honey-blond hair was down for a change. The strands tickled his cheeks.

"You'll find honesty turns me on."

"Good to know. Why do you have two bags?"

"Gorgeous and observant." He handed her the smaller of the two bags. "This one is for you."

Her eyes lit with excitement, her smile broadening. Rather than walk the garment bag to the couch and pull down the zipper, she did so standing on the steps.

"A coat!" She discarded the bag at her feet and held the puffy, down-stuffed orange coat to her chest. "I love it! Did you pick this out by yourself?"

"Yes," he lied. "Sort of."

"I *adore* it." She threw her arms around his neck and gave him another kiss. His hand to her back, he held her against him.

"If I knew you'd react this favorably, I'd have bought you another pair of Jimmy Choos, too."

"You're sweet." She finished him off with a final smooch. "I can finally go outside for longer than three minutes. I tried to watch the snowfall from the porch, but my leather coat was no match for the temperature. Now I can go outside in my new boots and my new coat."

"Oh, you're going outside, all right."

Her curiosity was almost as cute as her excitement. Hell, no it wasn't. The excitement was far better. It gave him all sorts of ideas about surprising her with more gifts. Avocados, as soon as the market had them back in stock. Or another pair of shoes. Wildflowers from the hillside out back. Then he remembered she wouldn't be here come spring. The thought was sobering for myriad reasons. The least of which was a timeline ending with her in LA and him in Dunn. The lion of which was how he'd mentally pictured a future with her when one didn't exist.

"Are you throwing me out or something?" She poked him in the chest and he snapped back to the present.

"I'm going to show you what I'm filming. Only not up there." He nodded in the direction of his office. "In real time. We're going on a little nature hike. You interested?"

"So interested." Her enthusiasm made it tough for him to hide how pleased he was to hear it. So he didn't hide it. He grinned, teeth and all, letting her see right through to his soul. "I'll pack some snacks."

"Food. Of course you're preparing food. I'm going to hang this up." He tromped upstairs and pulled open the doors to his closet. It was a large space with plenty of room for everything he needed. And more, apparently. On a rod on the immediate left of the closet that used to hold his unused suits hung frilly shirts and slim jeans, a black dress and the rest of Kendall's belongings. Her new Choos, along with the open-toed boots she'd worn the first time he'd seen her, sat on a shelf below.

He hung his tailored suit on the rod where she'd moved his other suits, pausing again to take in the sight of a woman's clothes in his closet. Once upon a time Bunny had hung her clothes in this closet. That had been the last time he'd shared the intimate space.

With his ex-wife, intimacy was a challenge as well as a massive adjustment. Especially when she constantly consolidated his clothes to make room for more of hers. Same as Kendall had done, except for one glaring difference.

Max didn't mind.

He didn't mind her being here, sharing his bed, trimming his hair—though they'd gone another round about his beard before he made her swear not to touch it. Her clothes in his closet, her sitting in his spot on the couch, or putting his spices back into the wrong kitchen cabinets.

After the divorce, he had relegated himself to the idea of being a loner who preferred privacy over companionship. That'd been two years ago now. He wasn't sure if he'd gotten over longing for privacy, or if he'd never truly wanted privacy, but just needed to be away from Bunny.

This thing with Kendall was more than scratching an itch or recovering from being lonely. He wanted to please her, wanted to help her. Her story about losing her brother had made him picture a frightened little girl with big hopes and dreams for a future. If he could help her dreams come true, why wouldn't he?

"Sorry about that." He heard her before he saw her. She stepped into the closet with him and gestured to her clothes. "They were starting to wrinkle in my suitcase. I can move them if—"

He swept her against him and kissed her hard, slipping his tongue into her mouth and making out with her long and slow. When the making out moved to his hand beneath her shirt and his other hand on her ass, she was moaning and begging and murmuring his name.

"I'm forgiven, I'm guessing." Her lips were swollen from his beard, pink and inviting.

"You don't have to be sorry for making yourself at home." When that sounded too mushy, he added, "Feel free to slip out of those clothes and make yourself extra comfortable."

"You first." She unhooked his belt and slipped the thick leather through the loops of his jeans. Then she started on the buttons of his shirt. "Try on your suit for me."

"My birthday suit?"

"You know which suit I'm talking about."

"I'm not putting it on again. Not until we shoot footage for the commercial."

"But I want to see it."

He pressed a kiss squarely onto the center of her lips. *"No."*

"I like you better when you're agreeable. Like when I was cutting your hair."

"You had a pointed object close to my head."

"Well, you have a pointed object in your *pants*." She cupped his shaft and stroked him through his jeans. He sucked in a short breath and promptly forgot what they were arguing about. "Pants I'm about to remove."

She kept her word, and soon he was out of his jeans and shrugging off his shirt. He'd just dropped the chambray to the floor when she did the same. On her knees, she peered up at him, her hand still wrapped around his favorite part of his anatomy.

"I've been wanting to do this," she announced with a question in her smile.

"Knock yourself out, California."

"You're into it."

He let out a sharp laugh. "Is there a man alive who isn't?"

"Probably not." Rather than debate further, she kissed the tip with her warm, wet mouth. His eyes rolled back in his head when the kiss turned into a lick and the lick turned into a suck. Soon he was engulfed by her mouth. Her suctioning cheeks and that—right there—whatever she had just done with her tongue.

He rested a palm on her head and wound his fingers in her hair when she did it again. He tried to tell her he liked it but a hissed breath through his teeth was all he could manage. Thank God she read his nonverbal clues. She didn't slow down, didn't let up. She sank deep and pulled away, only to sink deep again. He ended up half-buried in his shirts, one hand on her head, the other hand gripping one of the shelves for stability. His stability. Watching her take him into her mouth and let him go would be forever seared into his memory. A memory that wouldn't include him collapsing on his ass because she'd taken him all the way.

"Enough," he growled, incapable of more words at the moment. He tightened his hand in her hair as she eased off him, and he memorized the shape of her mouth as it left his glistening length. He blinked hard and tried to shake the vision. Impossible. It was riveted to his brain—for better or worse. He'd better last more than a few hot seconds or he was going to be well and truly pissed.

Kendall rose to her full height, and the second she was within reach he took off her clothes. Sweater. Gone. T-shirt. Gone. Belt. Gone. Jeans. Socks. All gone. When she was gloriously naked before him, he lowered her to the carpeted floor of the closet and entered her with one smooth stroke.

Her eyes were on his, her mouth open. She lifted her hands to thread into his hair, frowning when there wasn't as much to hold on to as before. "I liked you shaggy." He rolled his hips and thrust into her. "That feels good."

"My hair'll grow." Not that she'd be here when it did. He shut out the thought and focused on her tight heat gripping him, and the feel of her hands in his hair, moving over his shoulders, smoothing over his chest. It'd been too long since he'd been touched with such affection. Not in haste to reach joined orgasms and then part ways, more a fascination to discover something new.

Something new. That's what he'd found in Kendall.

At one point he'd decided he'd left an old version of himself in Hollywood. A former version he no longer consorted with. And then came Kendall, making LA seem new again. Making him feel new again.

He hooked her leg over his hip and sank deep. She threw her head back, shouting when an orgasm washed over her. He absorbed the shock waves as she milked his release from him without trying. He came hard, propping himself onto his elbows so he wouldn't crush her beneath him. His fingers were nested in her hair, that soft, soft hair. His lips were on her cheek. Her soft, soft cheek.

He concentrated on her softness. On her slower, longer breaths. On the feel of her fingertips gliding over him as they would the delicate fringes of a feather instead of a flesh-and-bone man who'd just taken her on the floor of his walk-in closet. Tender touches were a lost art in his world. Hookups were fast, rushed. From what he remembered anyway.

"Thanks for the coat," she rasped. She was flushed and smiling, her hair tangled, her eyelids open halfway.

Through a rough chuckle, he said, "Remind me to buy you gifts more often."

"Remind me to snoop more often."

"You don't need reminding for that."

A shadow swept over her face, altering her sated, spent state and trading it for something darker. He wasn't sure if he'd let his thoughts show on his face. Though, the sex had spoken for itself, hadn't it?

No matter what it looked like on the outside— hasty closet sex—he and Kendall had connected. He knew better than to connect with anyone, but this woman had cracked him open and found his gooey caramel center. It was dangerous. It was stupid. It was—

Her lips touched his gently as she stroked his cheek with her thumb. Her dark eyes were deep and twinkling—as if they hid a million secret galaxies.

"That was—" she started.

"Worth it," he finished for her.

"That's a new one." She smiled softly.

It sure as hell was. No matter what it cost him personally to agree to the commercial, or to have her in his life for a limited time, or to awaken the part of himself he'd thought he'd buried for good, he knew deep in his gut…

Time spent with Kendall would be worth every second of turmoil that inevitably followed.

Fourteen

"So, tell me what's doing," were the first words out of Meghan's mouth when Kendall answered her phone. "How was your trip to Virginia? You didn't call me once, and it's been almost a week. I'm feeling neglected."

Kendall, in the middle of pulling on her winter boots for a wilderness hike with Max, bristled. She hadn't meant to keep her sister in the dark, but she'd been preoccupied. And yes, a *little* nervous to call her sister and admit what she'd been doing....and whom she'd been doing it with. But she could use someone to talk to, even if it meant admitting she'd bent the truth for the sake of her and Isaac's careers.

Then there was the line she'd crossed with Max. What had started out as a fun kiss in the hot tub, and had advanced to the bedroom and beyond, shouldn't and *couldn't* turn into anything more. Meghan would understand, and she would be a voice of reason.

"It's an interesting story," Kendall started. She really didn't know *where* to start. She wasn't too shy to tell her sister about her sex life, but Kendall's secret affair was a secret, and she was finding she liked it that way.

"I love interesting stories! Can it be on the record? I've been wanting to interview you about what it was like to meet Max Dunn. You don't have to share details of his private life, obviously… Well, can you share a teeny bit of his private life?" Meghan giggled at her own chutzpah. "I'm dying to know what he's like. Is he half as attractive as Isaac?"

"Oh yeah," Kendall answered without hesitation. Max was downstairs packing up camera equipment, but just in case he could hear her, she stood and shut his bedroom door. She sat down on the bed and lowered her voice to be doubly sure. "I kind of… haven't left yet."

"You're still in Dunn, Virginia?"

"My car was stuck in the snow after a minor car accident—"

"A car accident!"

"I'm fine, I promise. I ended up hiking in the snow back to Max's house because he was closer than going to town." She felt her cheeks grow warm. "I'm staying in his cabin."

Meghan gasped, and a delighted peal of laughter

followed. "I cannot believe this. You are totally having sex with Max Dunn!"

Kendall couldn't keep up with the questions coming at her machine-gun style over the phone. Meghan asked who kissed whom first, if the sex was any good and if Kendall was planning to move to Virginia. She wrapped up by saying, "I'd love having you closer to me."

Kendall felt every syllable of her sister's request in her chest. She missed Meghan. She missed her parents. And if her brother was still on this planet, she'd miss him more than she did now. Some days California felt like a world away, but...

"Slow your roll, Meg," she warned with a smile. "This is as temporary as the blizzard. When the snow is gone, so am I." A dart of regret stabbed her chest. She ignored it.

"So the sex isn't any good?" Meghan's disappointment was evident.

"Are you kidding? If it was any better, I'd be comatose. I'm going to miss the sex the most."

Meghan laughed as Kendall had intended, but that wasn't true. What she would miss most was Max. She'd grown used to his calming presence. Whether he was building a fire, or chopping wood to build a fire—which was the sexiest sight—or he was complimenting her on the meal she'd cooked. Or he was scolding her about working too much, and telling her to take a break.

"I would trade my entire career to meet the Dunn brothers, and you are sleeping with one of them."

"You'll meet Isaac. Eventually. He's not in the country at the moment."

"You have been working for that talent agency for years, and I still haven't met him!"

"Yes, but now I'm *his* talent agent instead of an assistant, so you are totally going to have the chance to meet him."

"Plus you have an *in* with Max. When are you going home?"

"The mountain roads are blocked, though we can go to town and back without a problem. My rental car hasn't been repaired yet. I'll have to return it to the agency."

"Does this mean you lost your chance at the Citizen commercial?"

"Actually…" Kendall filled in her sister on what had transpired regarding the ad. How Max had refused, how Isaac was upset when Kendall learned the name of his private island—she was in no way sharing that info with Meghan—and then how, finally, Max offered to step in.

"What caused the change of heart? The fantastic sex?"

"No, this was before." Kendall smiled sadly. "I opened up about Quin, talked about my goals. I think he wanted to help." The way he wanted to help her with everything. Her car, keeping her warm and dry by buying her a coat, his seemingly endless need to delight her in the bedroom. "Today we're going on a hike."

"In the snow?"

"Crazy, right? He bought me a coat so we could—"

"He bought you a coat?" Meghan's tone took on the consistency of melted chocolate. "I knew it. I knew the internet lied about Max. The gossip sites say he's washed up and rude, since he refuses any and all interviews, and that he's difficult to work with. Unless he is those things and you have the magic touch."

A slightly terrifying thought. "It's not like that. And to answer your earlier question, I'm not moving to Virginia. My home is in Los Angeles, Max's home is here. You know I'm not interested in settling down."

"Because of Quinton," she said with calm surety.

"Quinton?"

"He left all of us, Kendall. But you were the only one who walled yourself up so you'd never be left again."

"I didn't wall myself up." Kendall stood from the bed and paced to the window, irked by her sister's assessment. She hadn't shut down, she simply wasn't looking for a permanent relationship. Was that so hard to understand?

"I respect you wanting to protect yourself, Ken, but Quin would've wanted you to enjoy your life."

"I moved to California to do the very thing I wanted to do so I could enjoy my life. The thing he encouraged me to do." She didn't mean to sound defensive, but it'd crept into her tone anyway. "This has nothing to do with our brother. My visit to Dunn is as temporary as it ever was." Kendall couldn't help adding, "What makes you think Max would want me around any longer? After we shoot this commercial footage, I'm flying home. He knows that. It's not like every single person has to be paired up with a soul mate."

"Okay, okay. I didn't mean to touch a sore spot. As you recall, I am as hopelessly single as you are. Although, I would accept sleeping with one of the Dunn brothers on the temporary as a suitable exchange."

Using the excuse she'd be late for their hike, Kendall wished her sister well and wrapped up the call. Just in time, too. When she pulled open the bedroom door, Max was standing on the other side.

"You scared me," she said, but her heart thundered for a totally different reason. Talk of Quinton and walls and moving to Virginia... Meghan had been completely off base.

"Sorry about that." Max's expression was neutral, hinting he hadn't heard her saying whatever it was she said aloud. "I'm packed. You ready to go?"

"Yep! I was just talking to my sister. Ready when you are."

So, that was her sister on the phone. He'd wondered.

Max hadn't meant to eavesdrop, but when he arrived at his bedroom door—his *closed* bedroom door—he couldn't help listening in when he heard Kendall say she planned on taking the first flight out of town as soon as humanly possible.

Which was for the best. But he'd hoped she would

linger for another week or so. He wasn't above asking her to stay—even after he'd overheard her decision to leave. People changed their minds all the time. Look at him, preparing to act in a friggin' commercial.

They suited up, Max carrying his camera bag on one shoulder, and Kendall tucking her cellphone into her pocket. Beyond the back patio, the snow was knee-deep in some areas. For her anyway. It was shin-deep on him. In the few instances she struggled, he wrapped an arm around her waist and moved her into a shallower area. She joked about how there was probably a drift hundreds of feet deep she'd step in and never be heard from again. He told her she'd seen too many movies.

He'd set up feeding stations in the woods behind his house for deer, squirrels, foxes and black bears. He explained this to Kendall while he was filming B footage for their commercial.

"Black bears?" The snow crunched as she moved closer to him.

"They're a rare sight. Black bears are shy. Like I was in high school."

She waited until he lowered the camera to refute his claim, just as he figured she would.

"You didn't go to high school." Her words were a visible puff in the cold air.

"True. But I was shy."

"Which one of you kissed Rachael on-screen?" Kendall asked. "I've always wondered."

Rachael was a character written in toward the end of the show as Danny's love interest. By then,

Isaac and Max were fifteen, old enough to be on set—when they weren't in school—up to ten hours a day. Also, by then, Max had been counting down the minutes until he could return to some semblance of a normal life. Though he'd had no idea what "normal" looked like after having worked on a television set since age five.

"That was Isaac," he answered.

"Did you flip a coin?"

"No. He exuberantly volunteered."

Kendall laughed. "He really is the more outgoing one of the two of you, isn't he?"

"Yeah, but I'm a better kisser."

"Poor Rachael." She tipped her chin and pursed her lips. He bent to kiss her. Her cheeks were cold and so was her nose, but her mouth was warm and welcoming. After the light press of their lips, her eyes opened dazedly. "I like this."

"The nature walk?" he teased.

"Yeah," she confirmed, but the twinkle in her eye suggested she'd been referring to being close to him.

"I was thinking…" He fiddled with the camera settings rather than look at her, which made him feel like the shy version of himself he'd thought no longer existed. "I need a date to the awards dinner thing in town. Are you interested in coming with me?"

Her eyebrows climbed her forehead, nearly vanishing in her coat's fur-lined hood. He'd shocked her. And himself. He had planned on prefacing the ask by giving her a handful of reasons to say yes rather than charging in. Maybe warn her that even after the roads were cleared, they could still be treacherous. Or suggest she wait to fly out until the rest of the state wasn't also trying to leave Virginia. But it wasn't like him to dance around asking for what he wanted.

"I'm quickly running out of clothes, Max." Her smile was nervous. It was sweet. *She* was sweet.

"Why do you need clothes? I'll build an extrawarm fire every day."

"So you want me to stay for the sex."

"I want you to stay and come with me to the dinner, but the sex is a nice perk."

"What will your townspeople say?"

"They're not *mine*."

"They live in a town they named Dunn in honor of *you*. Trust me. They're yours." She poked him with a gloved finger. Then she studied the mountain range in the distance. They'd hiked to the overlook, which was surrounded by tall pines and dipped into a valley with a currently frozen stream. "It really is beautiful out here."

"LA's got nothing on this view." He let her change the subject. He wasn't going to try to talk her into staying if she couldn't. She didn't live here. She had a job: agenting his brother. And, as she had proclaimed repeatedly, she wasn't cut out for mountain life. Though he was starting to wonder. Whether she was curled up by the fire in her pajamas sipping hot tea, or in the hot tub admiring his enviable mountain view, she seemed to fit in his world just fine.

At least, for now.

"Why not," she said suddenly.

"Why not what?"

"'Why not' was my way of saying yes to your invitation. No sense in rushing out of here, right? Especially when the sex is this good."

"So you're agreeing to the dinner, and more incredible sex together?" He wasn't 100 percent sure he could be that lucky.

"The dinner is the least I can do to repay you for the commercial. And the coat. Like you said, the sex is a perk."

"You don't have to repay me for the coat." He gave her another warm-cold kiss. "But I'll accept your *yes* to both the dinner and the sex."

Fifteen

"And then I'm supposed to take off your shirt," Kendall read from her email.

"Take off my shirt?" Max's hands halted over the knot in his tie. He was wearing the suit they'd picked out, and damn did he look good in it. He'd looked good in it the day they bought it, but now that it was tailored to fit him perfectly, he was practically edible.

"'Unbutton Isaac's shirt, run hands over his chest,'" she read aloud. "Wow, that was awkward."

"Imagine if I were actually Isaac." His beard was trimmed to perfection—by him, he hadn't let her touch it, though she'd offered. His hair was wavy and neatly styled against his head.

"Ew, no." She grimaced.

"I'm glad to hear you say that. When you were

first stranded here, you were going to fly to his island and make this happen."

"Yes, but not with *me*. With Natasha Tovar, the model." And Kendall, while she was a former Miss North Carolina, was no Natasha Tovar.

She had given herself several pep talks since she and Max returned from their hike. She'd showered and dressed in her new Choos and the formal black dress she'd brought. Once she'd applied her makeup and rolled her hair into fat waves with a curling iron, she was feeling more, not less nervous. She was beginning to question her own assurances that she'd be a backdrop no one would notice. Rolling around on the couch with Max off-camera was one thing. This... this was a whole other thing.

She turned to find him adjusting the tripod. It was facing the sofa, which he'd angled so the fireplace was in the background. Several blankets were thrown over the cushions for some of the more intimate shots.

"Start with the walk-in, right?" He adjusted the tripod for his height.

"Y-yes."

"Are you nervous, California?"

"A little."

He came to her, put both palms on her bare arms and rubbed. She tilted her chin up to look at him, drawing strength from his powerful presence.

"All you have to do is pretend you like to touch me."

She grabbed his tie and tugged. "You are such a smart-ass."

"The trick is to *almost* kiss me," he murmured, his lips close to hers, "but don't do it. We can practice if you want."

Her hand curled tighter around his tie. This close to him, all she wanted to do was *actually* kiss him and damn the commercial. She wasn't shy about that. The commercial was for Isaac's career and Citizen's success, and hers, as well. She had to get this right.

"Okay," she whispered. "Should I look at you?"

"The only time you shouldn't is when you close your eyes to enjoy what I'm doing to you. What I'm *almost* doing to you." His voice had dropped an octave or three. He winked, flashing her a wicked grin in the process. If his closeness, how good he smelled, or how great he looked hadn't done her in, his low voice would have.

"I can do this," she reminded both of them.

"Hell yeah, you can. I've got you."

She nodded. Once the footage was complete, she could forget about the commercial and move on. Which was as good an excuse as any to stay in the present with him.

"From the top," he instructed.

There were no spoken lines, but they had a script of sorts. He'd helped her map out each of the shots, and the production crew had supplied suggestions for the emotions they'd like them to act out. She adjusted her watchband and rolled her shoulders, reviewing the scenes in her mind.

Max, his back to her, out of frame, rolled his neck left then right. Then he turned around and those blue eyes burned straight into her. He was suddenly a bigger, bolder version of himself. Wearing the room like part of his outfit as he stalked toward her. His nostrils flared, his eyebrows slammed over his nose. She kept her expression in check while marveling on the inside how amazing it was to watch him transform into *Max the Actor*.

He folded his arms, keeping the watch visible. She tossed her hair with one hand, cognizant of her timepiece, as well. He advanced a step, reaching for her waist, anger shimmering off him in waves. It was so real, she had to remind herself he wasn't upset with her. This was an act.

Unsure in her own acting abilities, she decided to instead lose herself in Max. To pretend what he was doing was real and react in kind. She clutched his tie as she'd done before the camera was on, but this time tipped her head to the side and stared at his mouth. He came to her so slowly it was like time stood still.

Her heart thrashed in her chest when the mouth she wanted very badly to kiss bypassed her lips and went to her neck. His lips grazed the skin of her throat, but didn't close over her pulse point the way she wanted. She held onto him to keep from losing herself completely, but her eyes shut of their own volition.

He glided his lips from her neck to her jaw, and her next breath stuttered from her mouth. When he reached the apple of her cheek and finally her eyelashes, she was well and truly lost. He could lift her into his arms and take her anywhere and she wouldn't resist.

He spoke into her ear, his voice both gruff and gentle. "Nicely done."

She opened her eyes and found him smiling down at her. She was still half-lost in a hazy shroud of lust. And from a few "almost" kisses.

"Wow. You're very good." She didn't hide the awe in her voice—hell she still felt it in her bones.

"Thanks, California." He moved to the camera and pressed a button. "I hit Record just in case. I think you nailed it. But we can watch to make sure."

"Oh, oh. Yeah, I should probably approve that." Her laugh was self-conscious.

"It's your commercial. You can do whatever you want."

She walked to the camera and watched the tiny screen as he played back the footage. She tried to be objective, but it was impossible to separate the feelings being portrayed on screen from the actual ones inside her—mainly because they were identical.

"That was... honest." She swallowed thickly.

"Making people believe what you want them to believe is acting. That's all. Nothing else."

"And will they believe you're Isaac?"

Max's expression darkened a shade. "They'll believe whatever you tell them."

She nodded, nervous all over again. Would the world believe she was gone for Isaac after they watched this commercial? Because that was what it looked like.

"But you and I will always know the truth." Max wrapped an arm around her. "Ready to move to the couch? Take my shirt off?"

She laughed. "Are you sure you want to do this?"

"Too late to turn back now. Come on. Just like we've practiced over and over and over again. Only make sure you stop before you do something you don't want on film." He smiled easily, reset the camera and pressed Record. When he lounged on the corner of the couch, jacket off, arms wide and tie pointing down the center of his shirt, she decided to go with it.

When would she have a chance as unique as this one again? Never, that's when. Because she would never be in a commercial again—and not with Max. It was time to enjoy herself. During the commercial, and during the week leading up to the fancy dinner in Dunn.

Kendall lowered to the sofa, settled between Max's parted legs and began tugging at his tie. Then she unbuttoned his shirt while pinning him with dark eyes filled with want.

"Hold that thought," he growled when her hand rested on his bare chest. She'd settled on top of him, and thank Christ was blocking the hard-on he hadn't intended on displaying for the camera.

Sliding her with him, he moved them out of frame and stood. His chest heaved beneath his open shirt, hanging at his sides. She smiled up at him as she toyed with the tie he was no longer wearing. Then she crossed those long legs that were making him hornier than hell.

He shut off the camera and, to be double sure, capped the lens. He returned to the vixen on his sofa in two wide steps, and tossed her new shoes over his shoulder one by one.

"What's wrong?" she asked through a laugh. "Having trouble reining it in for the sake of the commercial?" She yipped when he grabbed her ankles and yanked. Once he had her flat on her back, he fisted her dress and shoved it to her thighs. Her gasp of excitement spurred him on.

He'd never before popped a woody during filming. While he hadn't participated in the first on-screen kiss with their love interest on the show, he had participated in a few. On-screen kisses were awkward. Strange. And being observed by an entire crew. In this case, however, it was just him and Kendall and he was having a hard time remembering this was pretend.

Kendall, slinking over him in her tight dress. Kendall, playing her fingers delicately on his bare chest. Kendall, poised perfectly, waiting for him to guide her so she could react to his next move.

The more he interacted with her, the more compatible they seemed to be. At first he'd assumed she was like Bunny: self-serving, prioritizing her needs before anyone else's and damn the consequences. But Kendall wasn't like his ex-wife. She was soft and giving, and she was looking out for everyone in the process. Even her ambition was connected to someone else—her brother who'd believed in her and had encouraged her to chase her dreams.

Max placed an openmouthed kiss on her thigh and shut out any thought apart from making her moan his name in ecstasy.

"I thought you were pretending to be turned on," she breathed, her hand nested his hair.

"No one can pretend that well," he mumbled against the soft skin of her inner thigh. He wanted her. Badly. But first he would wring an orgasm from her lush body.

"You're a pro." She continued mangling his carefully styled hair.

He kissed his way up to the apex of her thighs. "You ain't seen nothin' yet."

She laughed, but the sound was soon lost on a sigh of surrender. Just what he wanted to hear.

Hands gripping her thighs, he settled in to feast on her, licking and laving. He chased her when she couldn't hold her hips still, homing in on one spot in particular when she cried out the word *yes*. And when she advanced from "yes" to "yes, Max," he knew she was close.

Her orgasm rocketed through her, her body riding a wave up to his mouth and down again. Only then did he push to his knees and undo his pants. She reached for him, her teeth spearing her lip, her eyes barely open, her curls spread on the pillow behind her.

"You are a beautiful sight, Kendall Squire," he said as he eased past her folds and into the heart of her. She lifted her hips, wrapping her legs around to cradle him.

"I'm going to miss this when I go back to LA," she said, her eyes opening a little wider like she hadn't intended to admit that truth.

But there was no denying it. What they'd built together, even if it wasn't meant to last, even if it was only physical, was definitely unforgettable.

And so he told her as he sank deeply again, "Yeah, me, too."

Sixteen

Kendall insisted on buying a different dress for the awards dinner. Max agreed to let her borrow his truck to go shopping, but only after joking she should "try not to run it into a tree."

He'd pay for that.

A smirk was still on her face when she stopped at Luxury Bean, the coffee shop in town. Thanks to the late night spent sexing each other up, down and sideways, the one cup of coffee they'd enjoyed together this morning hadn't cut it.

The snow hadn't melted, but had finally stopped falling. Kendall easily found a cleared parking spot and pulled in, right in front of Luxury Bean.

"Help you?" an older woman asked from behind

the counter. She had sharp, high cheekbones, a slim waist, and short hair that suited her bone structure.

"Caffeine, please," Kendall said with a smile. "What's the best you have?"

"That would be my dark roast. I like to add steamed oat milk and a caramel syrup, but that's me." The woman pointed to the menu. "Or you can go with any of the espresso drinks. I can make 'em double if you like."

"I'll take your first suggestion…"

"Helen."

"Nice to meet you. I'm Kendall. Thank you, Helen."

"You're welcome, sweetness. Wander around. I'll set you up."

Kendall left the counter to admire the sundries for sale in the small shop. From mugs with *Brooks Knows Best* and the town name of Dunn on them, to bags of coffee boasting the Luxury Bean logo, there was a lot to peruse. Before she could choose which mug to purchase for herself, her phone rang.

Seeing it was a video call, she ran a hand through her hair and then pressed Answer. Isaac's face filled the screen—he was tan, with scruff on his jaw and chin like he hadn't bothered shaving. He looked so much like Max it was oddly alarming. Only when he opened his mouth, did the illusion fade—they sounded so incredibly different from each other.

"What's this about Max?" he asked, skipping pleasantries.

"I see you finally read my email. Took you long enough."

"Immersion, Kendall." Behind him, the waves rolled into the sand and a palm tree waved it's feathered fronds in the ocean breeze. "How the hell did you talk him into it?"

"I didn't. He offered to stand in as you and film the commercial. You should be grateful. He saved the Citizen contract."

"I suppose he won't accept payment for the gig."

"He might. If you offer. He did it for you, after all," she fudged. Max said he'd done the commercial for her, but she wasn't going to tell Isaac that. "Can I call you later? I'm in the middle of something."

He squinted at the screen. "Is that snow behind you? Where are you? Not still in Dunn."

"Yeah, I'm stuck here for the next week or so."

"Well, have Max take you to the airport as soon as the weather clears. You don't have to stay there with his grouchy ass because he agreed to do a commercial for me."

"Right." She forced a smile.

"Can't wait to see the ad. When's it done?"

"We have the footage we need, but they're not going to edit and release it for months. You might want to grow a beard by then. The world will need to believe Max is you."

"People believe what you tell them to believe, Kendall. Remember that."

Verbatim what Max had said on the subject.

Isaac told her to stay warm and signed off. She tucked her phone into her purse and, head down, nearly plowed into a blonde who was standing really, really close.

"Bunny?"

"Hi. Kendall, right? You were talking to Isaac."

Shit. She sure was. She was talking to Isaac about Max pretending to be him in a huge commercial that would air in a few months. Was it too much to hope Bunny hadn't overheard that part?

"How in the hell did you talk Max into doing a commercial?" Bunny lifted a mug from the shelf and checked the price tag on the bottom. "He hates acting. He hates Hollywood. I'm sort of surprised he's letting you stay with him."

"Oh, I'm—"

"No need to explain. I know exactly what Max is like. We were married, after all."

"Kendall," Helen interrupted, deliberately Kendall guessed. "Your coffee, darlin'."

"Thank you." Kendall sidestepped Bunny, anxious to make a hasty retreat. She didn't want to talk about their marriage, or about the switcheroo she'd talked Max into. But before she could escape, Bunny blocked the exit with her tiny body.

"Have a cup of coffee with me. I promise to be nice." Bunny turned to Helen. "My usual."

Helen nodded, her mouth tight. Kendall sent a longing look to the door over Bunny's shoulder before deciding to hear her out. Dunn was a relatively small town. She'd have a hard time avoiding Max's ex for the next week anyway.

"Sure," she told Bunny. "Why not?"

Two hours later, Kendall walked into the cabin with her dress. Max looked up from the kitchen counter, knife in hand. "I was about to send out a search party."

"Sorry. Finding a dress was harder than I thought."

"I knew you were all right, California. My truck is solid in the snow."

"Steak for dinner?" she asked as he trimmed the fat from a New York strip.

"And mashed potatoes." He pointed at the pot boiling away on the stove. "Did you find what you wanted to find?"

She hugged the garment bag to her chest. "I did."

"Why do you sound disappointed?"

"I ran into Bunny."

He set the knife aside and flattened his hands on the countertop. "Do I want to know?"

"She overheard me talking to Isaac at Luxury Bean. It's safe to say she figured out I'm not a hair stylist. She wants me to help her land a role on *Brooks Knows Best*. I explained to her I don't have the final say in who they cast."

"And." His voice dipped low, suspicion curling around the word.

"And I agreed to help her." Kendall shrugged and dropped her shoulders. She'd planned on leaving it at that and not telling him the rest, but the way he stared through her suggested he knew there was more. "She knows you're pretending to be Isaac in the commercial."

"Dammit." His beard tugged into a frown. "Did she threaten you?"

"Not exactly. She mentioned she was surprised you stepped in for him. But she didn't threaten me outright."

He shook his head and began trimming the steak again. "I'll talk to her."

"It's okay. I don't want you to worry about it." And she really didn't want him talking to his ex-wife. Not while Kendall was here. She supposed that was sort of juvenile, but she would rather have Max's undivided attention while she was in Dunn. When she left, he could contact his Bunny all he wanted. "The other reason I offered was to get her off your back, remember?"

"Kendall, I don't expect—"

"Let me help." She came to him and tipped her chin for a kiss. He gave her one, and chose not to say more. Though he did slide a look of annoyance down his perfect nose.

"I need to call Isaac back. I'll be off the phone by the time you have dinner done."

Kendall was pacing the living room, phone held in front of her for the video call. She talked to Isaac about everything from *Brooks Knows Best* to future opportunities and what he wanted to do next.

Max listened. It was impossible to keep from it since she was doing her pacing a few feet from where he was cooking. He ducked outside to light the grill, willing to brave the cold for a perfect steak, and then returned inside to hear his brother's voice.

"Let me talk to Max."

Kendall offered a wan smile. To save her the trouble of navigating an ocean of misunderstandings between him and his brother, Max held out a hand to take the phone.

"Isaac. How's the isle?"

"Eighty-three degrees and sunny. You should come out. Why you live on the side of a mountain freezing your balls off for half the year is beyond me."

Kendall picked up the garment bag she'd thrown over the back of the couch and jogged upstairs. Max figured to give him a chance to talk to his brother in private.

"She listening?" Isaac asked, reading his mind.

Max heard the shower turn on upstairs. "No."

"She's not your type."

Max bristled. Only Max knew Max's type.

"She's all business, and her business is Hollywood. Which you hate, in case you need reminding."

"I know Kendall better than you do."

Isaac ignored Max's growly warning and changed the subject. "How was shooting the commercial? Tell me what it was like to play the role of a lifetime—me."

Leave it to Isaac to fire the first shot.

"Funny enough, your name didn't come up." Max wasn't going to tell Isaac how sexy the commercial was, figuring it'd be better to let him see for himself. The production team would add sensual music and filters and edit it to appear even sexier, which would be quite a feat considering it'd been damn sexy already.

"How was Kendall?"

Mind stuck on sex, it took Max a second to realize his brother was inquiring about her acting abilities.

"A natural."

"Well, that's good." Isaac cleared his throat and looked to one side. Awkwardness crept in, as it often did whenever they talked. They used to have a lot in common, but now it was like they were on two different planets instead of in two different climates. Finally, Isaac spoke. "You deserve payment for the gig, Max. You'll be fully compensated. I'm not keeping money I didn't earn."

"I don't want the money. I did it for Kendall. She was in a tight spot, no thanks to you gallivanting off to your private island and leaving your work undone."

"I said no to the commercial," Isaac clipped. "I didn't leave anything undone."

"You didn't race home to help her out, either."

"I'm stuck here without a pilot! And you know why I won't tell anyone where I am. Where else can I go to be alone?"

"Dunn, Virginia," Max answered. "But you don't want to be alone. We both know it. You want constant coverage."

"This role means a lot to me. I can't afford to be

distracted by a stupid ad for a stupid watch company."

"Careful, brother, that's your sponsor you're talking about. You have to hock whatever advertisers want you to now. You're about to be a big deal again."

"It could have been us," Isaac said, anger etched in the lines of his face. Minus the beard, it was like looking in a mirror. "You were the one who said no to even a small part on the show. But you could have said yes. Said yes and worked with me again. Would it have killed you?"

It wouldn't have killed Max, not in the literal sense. But it would have taken a part of him he'd vowed never to give away again. A private part of him. "What can I say? I treasure my privacy, too."

"You treasure your privacy so much, you did a watch ad to thrust yourself into the spotlight," Isaac said with a grunt.

"No, baby brother," Max said to his seventy-two-seconds-younger twin. "I did a watch ad to thrust *you* into the spotlight."

Seventeen

Kendall took Max's hand as he helped her step from his truck to the sidewalk. The venue for the awards dinner was the very hotel she was supposed to have stayed in while visiting Dunn. Oh, how her plans had changed since then.

She stepped into the posh lobby and craned her head to take in a wide chandelier over deep gray marble flooring. If she would have made it to M hotel the day she'd arrived, she wouldn't have been disappointed. It continued to amaze her how this town managed to be both fancy and laid-back at the same time. The town of Dunn was more like Max than he would ever admit.

Speaking of Max, he'd been quiet since yesterday. She'd walked downstairs to reclaim her phone and had found him brooding at the fireplace, his mouth a firm line of displeasure. Though she'd given him privacy, it wasn't hard to guess he'd been arguing with Isaac. She couldn't help feeling as if their most recent disagreement was her fault. Especially since she was the one who had come here to convince Max to film the commercial in the first place.

He didn't seem upset with her when she'd curled up next to him on the sofa and stroked his hair. And he'd further proved he wasn't holding a grudge when he pulled her into his lap and set his lips to hers. They made out long and slow, losing their breath and losing track of time. They'd spent the remainder of the evening on the couch watching a forgettable movie.

They'd gone to bed late, both tired. Too tired to take the goodnight kiss to its inevitable end, and make love. Instead, she fell asleep in his arms, him playing the role of big spoon, which was her favorite role of his to date. He'd more than made up for their early night this morning, when he dived beneath the thick blankets and woke her with intimate kisses. They made love while the morning light grew steadily brighter, sifting in through the blinds and filling the room as the sun rose higher into the sky.

When it came time to dress for the awards dinner, Max had been in a better mood. At the last minute, he'd called Darnell with his measurements and asked for a tux. Darnell delivered it, insisting on following Max upstairs to ensure the fit was right.

It wasn't right. It was perfect. Every long line of Max's build was accentuated by superior stitching, as if Darnell was a painter rather than a tailor. Max, his shoulders squared off in the jacket, appeared taller and prouder. Kendall knew his tells though, and the tick in his cheek hinted he was attempting to hide a touch of nerves.

"This is a very nice hotel," she said as they strolled toward the main ballroom.

"I should have worn a suit," he grumbled before returning a wave to a couple across the room.

"You did wear a suit."

"I wore a *tux*."

She followed his gaze around the lobby and spotted more of Dunn's residents milling about. They were dressed in their finest, the men she'd spotted so far wearing suits rather than tuxedos.

Winding her arm around his, she reassured him, "You're the guest of honor. You should be in a tux."

He stopped short of the double doors leading into the ballroom to pass a gaze over her. "Once you put on this dress, I had to step it up. I realized a suit wouldn't cut it."

She slipped a hand down the bodice of her dress. It was bold purple, and if that wasn't dazzling enough on its own, sparkling stones were sprinkled along the waist and the short train. She had opted for simple diamond earrings—her standard—and had styled her hair into a chignon.

"I've been practicing for awards season my entire life," she told him with a smile. "I want an invitation to the big one ever so badly."

"This is a far cry from the academy, sweetheart."

An easy smile slipped onto his face as he cupped her waist. "Shall we?"

She nodded and he pulled open one of the doors to usher her in ahead of him. The room was filled with round tables dressed in white linens, the centerpieces consisting of white roses and gold candles. They were seated in the front, since they were guests of honor. Kendall tried not to marvel at the room as she took her chair. At each place setting was a card featuring a menu, the chef the one and only Bash Brambleton.

"Bash catered this event?" She waved the card at Max, who appeared amused by her being starstruck.

"He has a house in Dunn. Flies in and delights us with his culinary expertise on occasion. He must have been stuck here when the snow came. I can't imagine him flying in for this."

"Modesty is unattractive," came a thick French accent from behind them.

Her jaw dropped as she inclined her head at the older chef. He extended a hand, his signature star tattoos dotting his index finger, and offered it to Max. Then he shook Kendall's hand, and asked if she had any special requests for dinner. She told him she'd eat whatever he prepared and, before she could stop herself, referred to him as a gastronomic god. Max and Bash talked about the snow—Max was right. Bash had been stranded here—and caught up on local restaurant news. Then Bash wished Max well and said he'd be watching the speech from the kitchen.

"And you know famous chefs," she said after Bash left their table.

"Only the ones who come to Dunn," Max said. She decided then that Bash was wrong—she found modesty incredibly attractive.

When the guests were settled into their seats, dinner was served. Five courses of the most exquisite food Kendall could remember eating. At their table were councilmen for the city, and as luck would have it, Mayor Chambers and his wife—Bunny. Kendall was grateful they were seated at the opposite side of the table. She could feign politeness for one evening, but would rather not converse with Bunny more than absolutely necessary.

Once dessert was served, Max pushed away from the table. "It's speech time, California. You going to be okay here with my colleagues?"

"I'll watch out for her," said the director of public affairs, and all around very cool chick, Shelley Lipschultz. She was seated to Kendall's right and had been a fun conversationalist the whole evening. Bunny had sent the other woman a glare or three, but Shelley happily ignored her. Kendall did the same. "You just focus on not forgetting your speech."

"Impossible." Max stood and buttoned his jacket. "I didn't write one."

"I can't tell if he's kidding or not," Kendall said as he walked around to the back of the stage.

"If you can't read him, dear," Shelley said as she reached for her dessert fork, "then there's no hope for the rest of us."

The emcee, a man around Max's age, clean-shaven with thick sandy-brown hair, talked of Max's accomplishments. He showed photos on the screens on either side of the stage of Max as a young boy—many of them stills or promo shots from *Brooks Knows Best*. Kendall suffered a bout of nostalgia seeing photos of the Dunn boys. She remembered watching the show with her sister when she was growing up. She'd never had a crush on the Danny character the way Meghan had, but oddly enough, now she felt like she did.

Probably because of how much time she'd spent with Max. She might not know him well enough to know if he was teasing about writing a speech or not, but she knew him well enough to share his bed. She could also read his emotions, and she knew he liked a lot of black pepper on his steak. That had to count for something.

The emcee scrolled through more photos of the town of Dunn before Max moved here, and spoke about the various stages of construction that had occurred before it'd become what it was today: a beautiful, welcoming place where tourists and residents alike shared the streets in harmony. The emcee wrapped with a current photo of Max. The rugged, bearded former actor stood on his front porch in the summertime, one shoulder leaning on a column, his hands casually tucked into his front pockets. His blue T-shirt matched his eyes and his jeans were soft and worn. He belonged on the cover of *Architectural Di-*

gest—or an issue of *People*, next to the title "Sexiest Man Alive."

"And now," the emcee said, "please put your hands together for Max Dunn."

The ballroom erupted in applause as Max stepped onto the stage and into the spotlight. His smile was easy and his posture was relaxed. If any of his earlier nervousness was present, she couldn't tell. He clasped his hands and then rubbed them together, approaching the microphone stand with grace.

At times like these she couldn't reconcile his not wanting to be in the public eye. He was so damn good at it. Even now, as he lingered at the microphone, before he spoke the first word of his speech, the audience was riveted. Kendall included. He was too beautiful to look away from, too captivating to ignore.

"First, let me apologize for bringing tourists to your town," Max opened. The audience laughed on cue. "And second, thank you for letting me live here. For honoring me by naming your town after me, and for being the best damn friends and neighbors a man could ask for."

From there, he spoke of the years he'd spent looking for a community where he fit, and outlining his future plans for Dunn. At one point, Shelley leaned over and whispered into Kendall's ear that Max had prepared. "No one knows that many facts and figures off the top of his head," she said.

When Max finished his speech, he did so with another thank-you, and a promise to keep the improvements coming even if it did "draw in riffraff from California." He sent a sly glance Kendall's direction and she felt more eyes in the room go to her, as well. He wrapped his speech and then stepped off the stage to a hearty round of applause. He earned a few claps on the back during his walk back to his chair. He sat as the emcee took the stage to inform everyone that the formalities of the evening were over and to "please enjoy the band."

"Over already?" Kendall leaned in to ask Max. "No one else will take the stage to brag about Max Dunn's great accomplishments?"

"God, I hope not," he answered so sincerely she had to laugh. The band started up, a soft jazzy number, and he offered her his hand. "Dance with me?"

She blinked at his palm. The man was full of surprises. "Won't that draw attention?"

"To you in that dress? Probably. As long as the attention is off me, I'm all for it." He took her hand and stood, and then led her toward the dance floor.

Kendall felt people watching them, felt her own heartbeat slam against the walls of her chest. She had been with Max for a few weeks, but never out with him—not like this. She could only imagine what the guests of the dinner, a dinner honoring him, must be thinking. She accepted his hand and rested her other palm on his shoulder. He cupped her waist and began swaying.

"You're not half-bad at this," he commented as she kept time. "Did you learn to dance in preparation for the big awards ceremony you hope to be invited to?"

"You're making fun of me."

"I'm not." His eyes softened on hers. "You are beautiful in this dress, Kendall. You're beautiful out of it, too, but in it—absolutely stunning."

She tipped her head back and grinned. "I'm not sure how you managed to slip a compliment around a reference to me naked, but well done."

"Thank you." He grinned. "Did Bunny give you trouble?"

"Other than a few sour glances, no."

"She's a mayor's wife, so she's usually well-behaved. I'm still going to talk to her about what she said to you in the coffee shop."

"Don't worry about it. By the time the commercial comes out in a few months' time, I'll have her a gig booked somewhere, and she won't care anymore."

"Was Citizen happy with the footage?"

"Thrilled. They complimented your stellar camerawork. Or, well, Isaac's. I hope he's half as good as you if he's asked to direct in the future."

"He's better in front of the camera. That's where he wants to be."

She took a breath, recalling the brothers' tense phone call yesterday. "I'm sorry I put you in this position. I don't want to come between you two. No amount of money or success is worth that."

Max moved her in another smooth circle. "Not your fault, California. That rift existed long before you entered the picture. It's sweet of you to worry. Besides, it's worth it now that you're here with me tonight. Have you noticed everyone watching us?"

She hazarded a quick glance around the room to find plenty of eyes on them. "Yes."

"If you weren't here occupying my time, they'd take turns dragging me to the bar and congratulating me. Followed by giving me ideas for how we can improve the town."

"Seriously?"

"Seriously."

"You poor thing." She patted his cheek, his soft beard hair tickling her palm. "I'll protect you from the big bad townsfolk who love you too much."

He tightened his hold on her. "Have I ever told you how sexy you are when you're sassing me?" He didn't give her a chance to respond before he added, "It's been a long while since I've had a woman in my arms on a dance floor."

"Your wedding?" she guessed.

"We didn't dance." He let that statement lie a moment before continuing. "When I left LA, I swore never again to pull on a shiny pair of shoes, let alone a tux. And yet here I am, trying to be worthy of the woman who entered my life without warning."

Her next inhalation hovered in her throat as the crowd around them faded into the background.

"You make it easier to be seen, Kendall. I won't forget that. I won't forget *you*."

Eighteen

She was still soaking in the compliment when he lowered his head to kiss her. Her eyes closed on their own as she parted her lips.

When their mouths connected, he answered the unasked question on everyone's minds at the event. Were Kendall and Max romantically involved? No one would believe she was here as a professional courtesy. Not after he'd eaten her alive with his blue eyes all evening. And especially not after he'd held her close after kissing her.

There was also no way to deny what had happened in the brief time she'd spent in this mountain town with this mountain man. Oh, sure she'd tried denying it. She'd gone as far as emailing the agency with an updated schedule of when she would return to California, so she wouldn't be tempted to stay longer. It didn't help, though. She wanted to stay in Dunn, Virginia, with Max. Unless there was a chance he'd agree to be dragged back to LA, which she highly doubted.

She had done plenty of misguided, foolish things in her years as an adult. But falling in love with Max Dunn was the most foolish.

Not because he wasn't worth loving. He so totally was. It didn't matter that falling for her client's twin brother was ill-advised, that she'd have to figure out how to work remotely if she and Max were to have a chance at a future together, or the real biggie: that Max was as far from looking for more out of a relationship than sex as she was.

Thank God she was practical. She'd meant what she'd told her sister, Meghan, about not being interested in a long-term relationship. Sure, her heart might be trumpeting an announcement of love, banners flying as a parade marched down Main Street in her heart, but Kendall wasn't about to throw away her good sense.

She had a career to look after. It was more budding than blooming, but Isaac Dunn was a good actor to have on her roster. She might be reenacting her own version of *Jerry McGuire* by channeling her focus onto one client, but she refused to trot out a "you complete me" speech to Max. That would be insane.

The song wound to a close. Other couples parted and left the dance floor, but she and Max held on to each other. Until a petite dark-skinned woman waving her cell phone in the air shouted Max's name.

Helen from the coffee shop looked both confused and concerned as she thrust her phone into his hand. "I had no idea you filmed a Citizen watch commercial. Evidently it was leaked. You sure keep your secrets from us devoted townies, don't you?"

Helen blinked at Kendall before offering a small smile. "And you look beautiful in it, dear. Just ravishing."

"I didn't shoot a commercial," Max stated rigidly. "That's Isaac."

Kendall couldn't respond, not even to back up his false claim. Her mind was busy running in circles. "That commercial doesn't air for a few months."

"I assume that's what *leaked* means," Max muttered as he frowned down at the phone. Below the embedded video was a blog. He thumbed the screen, skimming the text.

"Well, I know the article says it's Isaac, but I have eyeballs. I know that's you," Helen said. "No denying the chemistry between you two!" She was 100 percent correct, but there was no way they could allow her to believe Max was the one in the commercial.

"That is your home here in Dunn," Helen continued, sounding unsure now, "right?"

Kendall held her breath. They were going to have some serious public relations issues to handle. The world believed the man in the video was Isaac, but the people who knew Max best might question it the way Helen had.

"Not my house, but that's Isaac. Sorry to disappoint." He handed the older woman's phone back to her.

"Isaac and I shot this months ago in LA," Kendall said, relieved to have found her voice. "That's a soundstage, believe it or not. Though we did use photos of Max's house as inspiration." She glanced around, noticing several other guests eyeing their phones, some of them leaning in to whisper to each other before glancing over at Kendall and Max.

"You're very believable in this commercial…with Isaac," Helen said carefully. "He looks *identical* to Max. Beard and all."

"Something I haven't been able to change since our births," Max grumbled, sounding unhappy about the attention.

"Isaac and I filmed the commercial before Max and I met. It's wild, isn't it, the way life works out?" Kendall curled her arm around Max's forearm. He was currently glaring across the room.

She followed his gaze to the blonde holding his attention. Bunny tossed her hair and offered a disingenuous smile. She then turned back to her mayor husband and Shelley, and leaned in as if sharing a secret.

"If you'll excuse—" Kendall started, but Max finished the sentence for her.

"Us." He clasped her hand and walked over to where Bunny stood. He didn't mince words or bother hiding his irritation when they arrived. "I need to talk to you," he told his ex-wife. "Shelley, why don't

you take the mayor to the bar for a drink. I'll join you in a bit."

"What's this about?" Greg Chambers asked, his mouth a displeased line.

"I'm sure it's about my future in Hollywood," Bunny answered. "Isn't that right, Kendall?"

"Y-yes." Kendall plastered a smile onto her face. "It's confidential. Max and I are sworn to secrecy."

"As you will be after our chat," Max told his ex-wife.

"If it's more of this acting nonsense, I can't be bothered. Shelley, let's refresh our drinks." Greg and Shelley made their way to the bar.

"I didn't leak the video, so don't start with me." Bunny folded her arms over a flouncy coral-colored dress.

"No, but you might leak the truth."

"Everyone here already knows the truth," Bunny said with a gleam of jealousy in her eyes. "It's so obvious it's the two of you drooling over each other in that footage."

"You're mistaken. I would think you'd know the difference between my brother and me. You and I were married for two years."

Bunny propped a hand on her hip. "I remember. Believe me. This room is packed with my husband's voters. You expect me to lie to them?"

"I expect you to audition for the role on *Brooks Knows Best* so we can solidify a contract," Kendall blurted out. "Is Mayor Chambers going to allow you to fly to LA to do it?"

* * *

His ex-wife's focus went from incriminating him to daydreaming of her future in Hollywood in a blink.

"Oh my God! Oh my God!" She squealed and then embraced Kendall in a big hug. "When? Where?"

"I'm in the process of setting it up. But they're interested. I swear to you if you breathe a word—"

"I won't. I promise. I'm not the vindictive sort," Bunny whispered, leaning closer. "I just want this so badly."

"I can't guarantee the role," Kendall insisted.

Max stared her down, trying to work out if she was lying. Kendall hadn't mentioned the possibility of his ex landing her dream role. It seemed like something she would have mentioned to him, at least casually.

"I'm in the process of securing an audition for you with Ashley Lee," Kendall continued.

Ashley was slated to be the director of the *Brooks Knows Best* reboot. Max didn't know her personally, but he'd heard she was married to producer Cecil Fowler's son.

"Oh my God!" Bunny shrieked again.

"You can't let anyone in Dunn believe that was Max in the commercial," Kendall whispered.

"Yes, but people know it's *you* in the commercial. Unless you are hiding an identical twin sister somewhere."

"I know they know it's me. The production company needed a stand-in. I have experience in the industry and I was available."

"So you want everyone to believe this is you and Isaac?" Bunny held up her phone and pressed Play on the seductive commercial. Set to music, and edited in sensual black and white with only the watches in gleaming color, it was the sexiest ad Max had ever laid eyes on.

And they'd have to sell the idea that Kendall was rolling around on the sofa with his twin brother. The thought made his blood boil. Bass thumped from the tiny speaker on the cell phone, as the video version of Max ran his lips along Kendall's neck.

Him. Not Isaac.

Max had been so damn smitten, he hadn't needed to pretend to seduce her. Then after they'd filmed, he'd seduced her for real.

"Something wrong, Max?" Bunny asked.

"It's Isaac in the video," he said through clenched teeth. "I didn't know Kendall when they shot it."

Bunny nodded her understanding that this was the story she was supposed to repeat. "The comments below the video are really something. Did you read them? The world is convinced Kendall and Isaac are an item. No doubt the paparazzi are checking every known address, past and present, for them."

"They won't find her here," Max said pointedly.

"They won't," his ex-wife said with an expressive head shake. "I wouldn't tell anyone, I swear."

"Good," Kendall chimed in. "My taking you on as a client requires trust."

Tears shimmered on the edges of Bunny's lashes as her mouth spread into a wide smile. "You're taking me on as a client?"

"I am. It's my job to make dreams come true."

"Thank you! Thank you, Kendall. Max." She beamed up at him, and for a moment he remembered what she was like when she wasn't chapping his ass. Her husband Greg returned, drink in hand, and caught her when she leaped into his arms. She whispered into his ear and his eyebrows climbed his forehead. He sent a look at Max as if to ask *Can you believe this?*

Frankly, Max couldn't believe *any* of it. Not that he'd starred in a commercial. Or that Bunny had finagled her way onto Kendall's roster—or that the entire town believed he was the one in the commercial instead of Isaac.

Which he was, but they weren't *supposed* to know the truth.

Max led Kendall away from Bunny and Greg, nodding at Shelley as he walked by. "Everyone in town knows I hate acting. Why would they assume I was in a commercial with you? They're supposed to believe what we tell them."

"Your neighbors are trusting their eyes. They saw us out on the dance floor, Max. It's painfully obvious what's going on."

His heart jumped as he considered what they'd been doing together, in private and a little in public. What they'd said—what they hadn't said. He'd put his ass on the line for Kendall, both in the commercial and in his personal life. He'd told her about his secret documentary. He'd showed her his world. In return, she'd made his life better, and as he'd promised her earlier tonight, he wouldn't forget her.

What he hadn't said was why he wouldn't forget her. He wouldn't have to since he wasn't willing to let her go. Technically, yes, she would fly back to her home in LA. But the world was connected by the vast internet and videoconferencing. Why did she have to live on the other side of the continental US to do her job? She could spend some of her time here on the East Coast with him. Her sister lived on the East Coast. Maybe that would be incentive enough for Kendall to stay here.

His house, his world was open to her. All he had to do was tell her how he felt. They'd started something together, even if it had been by accident. He didn't know what their lives would look like a month or a year from now, but finding out was worth the risk. He knew that much. He opened his mouth to tell her so, but she spoke first.

"I have to go back to LA as soon as possible." Her proclamation totally threw off his timing.

"Why?"

"Isaac's world is going to blow up, if it hasn't already. He's going to need to fly home and I'm going to need to be there to handle the offers that will come pouring in."

Not liking the idea of her racing home to be there for his brother, he growled, "So, call him on the phone."

She patted his chest and offered a polite smile. "After the rest of the world catches wind of this commercial, rumors of my affair with Isaac's brother could tank his career."

Max felt his nostrils flare. Once again, Isaac's career was being put ahead of Max's needs. Years ago, Max had wanted a normal life away from the bright lights of Hollywood. Isaac had eyes only for the glitz and fame. It seemed not much had changed, and now Kendall was showing her true colors, as well. She was Hollywood through and through, serving the machine instead of exploring what she could have here, with Max.

"Who gives a shit what people say?"

"Isaac," she said, driving a knife into Max's belly. "And me. And you should care, too. You want to be left alone? News of my whereabouts won't help you in that endeavor."

Nineteen

Morning arrived and brought with it memories of last night. How Helen had run in waving her cell phone and proclaiming Max was the star of the commercial, how Kendall had offered Bunny professional representation to distract her. How Kendall had slipped into business mode immediately, and told Max she needed to leave his house as soon as possible. It'd been the wrong thing to say to him… and at the wrong time. She hadn't meant to panic when she'd learned of the leaked footage but that's exactly what she'd done.

On the drive home, she'd brought up Bunny again, and had voiced her concern. He had assured her his ex-wife's words "held no venom."

"She's a pain in my ass, California, but she

wouldn't do anything to hurt me." He'd been quiet the remainder of the drive home, which was just as well. She'd had no idea what more to say to him—if anything.

Back at the cabin, he'd taken her coat and purse and set them aside.

"I'm going to bed," she'd announced, angling toward the stairs. Her feet had hurt from her high heels and she was overwhelmed by the three thousand things she'd have to do come morning.

"I don't think so." He'd positioned himself between the staircase and her person, his arms folded. "I'm through pretending. No one can see us now, so I'll do as I damn well please."

She'd never thought of herself as a woman who'd allow a man to toss her over his shoulder, swat her ass and carry her off to bed, but that's exactly what she'd allowed Max to do last night.

Dammit, she really did like him. *Loved him*, technically. She needed to get a handle on that and fast. She couldn't stay in Dunn and pretend the rumors about her and Isaac would blow over.

By late morning, she'd nearly convinced herself she had a handle on her heart, as well as the PR nightmare she'd have to contend with when she flew home. Blog after article after social media post crowed about the new "it" couple, Isaac and Kendall. Max wasn't going to like it. Not one bit.

He'd climbed out of bed before her, told her he was going outside to split wood and hadn't come back yet. She was downstairs in front of the fire he'd built, laptop and cell phone at the ready in case more bad news came in.

Everyone knew who she was, which admittedly was her intention when she'd moved to LA. But she'd wanted to be known for her amazing skills as a talent agent, not because she was the purported romantic interest of an actor.

Max was upset, but not because the people in town thought it was him in the ad, and he'd been forced to lie and say it wasn't. No, his anger seemed to stem from the fact everyone believed Isaac was the man who'd run his lips down her neck. Honestly, she couldn't blame him. She never could have done anything like that with Isaac. Only Max.

Her phone rang, jerking her from her thoughts. Citizen watches. She gulped as her heart zoomed to her toes.

"Ray, hi." She heard the timidity in her voice, so she cleared her throat and tried again. "It's good to hear from you!"

"Kendall Squire," the young CEO said. Was that a warning she heard in his tone? He let out a laugh next, so apparently not. "God, I *love* the internet. You can't buy publicity like this. God bless the influencers, too. They can't stay away from gossip. I guess you were wrong about them not noticing the woman in the ad, huh? You might want to polish up your résumé for a few more commercial gigs yourself. Ha!"

"Oh, no. No, no," she said through a nervous laugh. "I only stepped in out of desperation."

"The world loves you two. *We* love you two. How soon until you're both back in LA?"

"Soon. But, uh—"

"Good. Tell Isaac you'll be coming straight to our offices once you're settled. Schedule it with my assistant. We're going to make bank on your coupledom."

"Our...coupledom?"

"Don't dream of denying it. It's all anyone can talk about. Hell, I don't care if it's real or fake. With the attention the ad has drawn, we're looking at tripling our last quarter's sales. Especially after the photos at some fancy dinner surfaced."

"Pardon me?" Her heart had made the return trip up her body. It was now pounding in her throat.

"You and Isaac. At the big to-do in Max's honor. I don't know how you did it, but having him step in and pretend to be Max at the dinner was genius. I guess you didn't have much of a choice, though, since Max Dunn is the least cooperative man on the planet. Everyone knows he'd die before he gave a speech at a dinner in his honor."

She was still processing the first thing Ray had told her. "There are photos from last night?"

"Hell yeah, there are. Come on. You have to have known. You were practically making out on the dance floor."

Oh God.

She hadn't known. She hadn't been thinking about photographers or the commercial when she'd been falling in love with Max Dunn on that dance floor.

And she couldn't tell Ray that Max was the man

she was kissing—she couldn't tell anyone. Everyone in Dunn knew she had shown up with Max and not Isaac, but after seeing how loyal they were to Max, she couldn't imagine them breathing a word of the truth. Not that anyone would believe the truth at this point.

The public would much rather have a lie if it was the juicier option. Nothing was more interesting than a secret affair between an actor and his agent, caught snogging at a dinner party.

"I didn't know," she said woodenly as she did a frantic internet search on her laptop.

"Well, no matter. Keep doing what you're doing. It's great for business. For all of us. Citizen wants to film a few more follow-up ads featuring Isaac in the future. With you, of course."

"Like I said, that was a one-off."

"It won't work without you, kid." Ray sounded happy, likely picturing dollar signs. He ended the call after letting her know he'd be sending over contracts for her to review, and that he'd be including one for Isaac *and* one for her.

Max stepped in through the back door, his face red from the cold. The snow hadn't melted, though the roads had been cleared. Now she and "Isaac" could fly back to Los Angeles. Ray didn't seem interested in sharing their whereabouts with anyone, and why would he be? He was angling for more exclusive footage for future ads.

Citizen watches had paid generously for Isaac to be in their commercial. With the attention on them now, she could negotiate an even bigger fee for his participation. But there was no way she'd be in another ad with him—especially if Ray expected it to be as sexy as the first.

She finished typing *Isaac Dunn + Kendall Squire + Awards Dinner* into the search bar and pressed Enter.

Then she gasped aloud.

"What the hell?" Max roared when he saw what Kendall had pulled up on her computer screen. A photo of them on the dance floor, holding each other close, kissing. Another of them smiling at each other like no one else in the room existed. Clearly, someone with a camera had existed, and had aimed it right at them. He'd been too distracted to notice.

"Bunny?" she asked.

"No. She was on the opposite side of the room. This angle is from the direction of the bar."

"The bartender." She turned dark, worried eyes up at him. "How'd he know?"

"He probably saw the commercial leak like everyone else and decided to cash in. Hell, he probably doesn't live in town." Max lowered onto the sofa next to her and leaned over to read the article. The more he read, the more pissed off he became. "They think Isaac is pretending to be me?"

The reasons stated in the article were ludicrous. Everything from Max's miserly living situation to drug addiction was mentioned.

"This is bullshit." He shut the lid of her laptop. She reopened it.

"I need to book a flight right now. The mechanic can return my rental car and bill me." Under her breath, she added, "I'll have plenty of extra money now that Citizen wants another commercial deal."

Max felt the blood drain from his face. "With Isaac, I assume."

"Who else? We're a big hit." She didn't sound pleased, but she also didn't sound like she was angry enough to spit nails, which Max was.

"Before you—" was as far as he got before someone knocked on the door. Three swift *knock-knock-knocks*. He doubted Bunny would confirm her audition time in person. He yanked open the front door, seeing red the second his eyes landed on his brother's face.

"Isaac?" Kendall said from behind Max. "What are you doing here?"

"I should be asking you the same question. Why aren't you at home, handling this mess?"

She brushed by Max to grab his brother's arm, and dragged Isaac inside. "I have a million things to talk with you about. I don't know where to start."

"Let's start with us being romantically involved and go from there." Isaac sent a glare over his shoulder at Max. "It seems your moonlighting as an actor has blown up in a big way, big brother."

Twenty

It was hard to concentrate on the topic at hand with Max looming over her. She and Isaac were seated at the kitchen table, Max leaning on the island, arms folded, taking turns glaring at Isaac and then her.

Isaac seemed impervious to his brother's leering as he listened to her explain how the photos had surfaced, and how Citizen felt about them.

"I'm fairly certain the watch company, who sent over a contract for more ad spots for you, by the way, released the commercial themselves."

Isaac appeared mildly amused. "Sounds about right."

"You're not upset?" *She* was upset. Not at Isaac, but at the idea of Citizen using them. They'd set the expectations, made plans on a drop date for the ad. Then they changed everything without telling them—without telling *her*. She wouldn't be surprised if they'd planted the photographer/bartender at the dinner themselves.

"Haven't you heard of the term *no bad press*?" Isaac smiled. Max growled. "Don't start." To Kendall, he said, "I had a voicemail on my phone from Citizen, and they mentioned they were thrilled about the ad and couldn't wait to re-sign me. I arranged for the first flight here. If we're supposed to be seen together, we'd better start now."

She swung around to find Max glaring only at Isaac now. She felt partly—if not mostly—at fault for this new wrinkle in their relationship.

"I see one of two ways forward," she told Isaac. "Either we don't respond to the rumors and continue going about business as usual, or..." She paused. Max wouldn't like her other suggestion.

"Or?" Isaac prompted.

"We give the public what they want," she said softly. "We pretend to date."

"No." Max's voice was a thunderclap of disapproval.

"This isn't up to you," Isaac told him. "This is up to Kendall."

"I—"

"Kendall is not dating you. For real or for pretend," Max interrupted.

"Are you willing to step up and claim to be the man in the video, Max? Your fans would love it." Isaac's lip curled.

"He doesn't want the attention," she said so Max

wouldn't have to. "He only agreed to film the commercial to help me out."

Isaac's eyes narrowed. He leaned back in the kitchen chair and snapped a look from his brother to her. "You weren't pretending in that video, were you? You two are actually—"

"What we were *actually* doing is none of your damn business," Max said.

"It's my business, all right. She's supposedly dating me, and the gossip online contends that I've been pretending to *be you*. Your dream came true, Max. You're one hundred percent out of the spotlight. The world believes you're a drug addict, or a drunk, or just a washed-up recluse."

"Not the world. Just a few trolls online," she couldn't help defending. She sent a smile up to Max, whose frown deepened.

"Regardless, Max's dream was to be left alone. All alone. It seems his wish has finally been granted."

Max did say being alone was what he wanted. He didn't want the attention. He didn't want to be bothered. It's funny how he'd purchased an entire town—surrounding himself with townsfolk who treated him like family. There was a tender side to him he liked to pretend didn't exist, but it did. She'd seen it repeatedly. It was the part of him she'd fallen in love with. A tenderness she hadn't felt from the opposite sex since her brother had encouraged her to chase her dreams straight to California.

"Kendall isn't going to be seen on your arm, having her picture taken and being shouted at by paparazzi."

"Kendall is my agent, and she knows what is best for my career."

"Because it's all about you," Max roared. "It's always been about you and what you want."

"No, Max." Isaac stood, squaring his shoulders in a standoff across the table from his brother. "You were the one who tore apart the Dunn twins. Together, we're whole—a unit. You were the one who left. Don't forget that."

"You never cared what I wanted. Your wants were always more important than mine. You seem to be doing fine without me."

"Same to you, brother," Isaac muttered, a glint of anger lighting his blue eyes. "We'll be out of your way as soon as we book the flights home. If you care about her career at all, you'll encourage her to play the role of my girlfriend. The press is good for the show, good for the agency. She has a shortage of clients. That will change when her name's on everyone's lips." He shot Max one final glare. "That would require you to put her before yourself, though. Think you can do that?"

"She doesn't want to be with you. Even if she's faking," Max said.

She felt his glare on the back of her neck, and drew in a deep breath before facing him. "Actually…"

A look of betrayal flashed across Max's features. She wanted to eat her words, but instead forced them out.

"It's not real. But it has to be this way, at least until we figure out the best way forward."

A shadow darkened Max's brow. "And the Citizen offer?"

"I'll have bigger offers to consider," Isaac said, coming to her rescue. "She won't have to take those ad spots. Unless you want to," he told her.

She said nothing, mainly because she wasn't sure how to tell Isaac there was no way she could rub against him, strip him of his shirt and offer her neck for a sensual brush of his lips. He was handsome—obviously, as he was Max's carbon copy—and he was a professional, but Isaac wasn't the problem. It was her. She would feel as if she were cheating on Max if she filmed that style of commercial with his twin brother.

"Unless you want to step back into the public eye," she told Max. "This is the way it has to be."

He leaned over her, palms flat on the table, his face inches from hers, and said nothing. She warred with herself, both wanting him to agree, and save her from having to lie to everyone, and wanting him to say no, and do what was best for him.

"Would it kill you to support someone other than yourself?" Isaac interjected. Max didn't move a single muscle, only continued staring down Kendall.

"Isaac and I won't have to pretend forever," she whispered, attempting to console him.

"How long?" Max asked. When she didn't answer, he asked again. "How long will you pretend you're in love with my brother?"

"Ideally, until the show starts filming in the fall," Isaac answered.

"That long?" she heard herself ask. Max vibrated with anger next to her.

Isaac shrugged. "You can see each other in private. As long as no one knows, there's no harm."

"Max?" She turned her hopeful gaze on him. This could be the compromise they were looking for.

"I pretend on screen," he told her, his voice low. "I don't pretend in my real life. If you're with me, you're with me. I won't sneak around because my brother's precious career is at risk."

"It's not only about my career," Isaac said. "It's about her reputation. The press will eat her alive if they believe she jumped from one brother's bed to the other."

Max moved so fast, Kendall felt her hair lift on the wind created by his big body. He wrapped a hand around Isaac's shirt and, teeth bared, issued a warning. "She will never share your bed."

Isaac, a good match for Max in strength and size, shook off his brother's hold. "I'm not going to sleep with her, you dumbass."

"No, but you'll pretend you are. While I sit here and watch it unfold online and on television."

"So do a walk-on for *Brooks Knows Best*," Isaac offered, his tone affable. "Get an apartment in LA, film for a few days and step back into the world you left behind. Tell everyone it was you in the ad, and claim Kendall for yourself. You care about her, clearly."

Her next breath was shallow as she waited and prayed for Max to admit he cared about her. Isaac had presented a third option she hadn't dared mention. Max had been clear about how he felt about Hollywood. But if he agreed to a small part on the show and returned to LA, they wouldn't have to pretend at all. She could be seen with Max all she wanted. Citizen might offer him future commercials. She'd film another one with Max, no problem.

"It's a great idea," she nudged. "You can stay with me. I could return the favor for you letting me stay here."

Max's face hardened. Her smile fell. He wasn't considering what Isaac said, what she was seconding with all her heart. He appeared to be measuring his reaction, maybe trying very hard not to strangle Isaac.

"I'm not selling pieces of myself to Hollywood any longer."

"Not even for me?" But she saw the answer on his face. It was a no that would surely destroy her heart. He was going to leave her on her own with no promise of returning. Much like her brother had.

"You walk out of this cabin with Isaac, California, he's the only Dunn brother you'll have claim to."

"Max, Jesus," Isaac tried.

"Same goes for you." Max poked Isaac in the chest. "You let Kendall be seen with you like you're romantically involved, you'll never hear from me again."

Isaac's face paled. "You don't mean that. Our parents. Christmas. What about—"

"I mean it. We survived fine without speaking to each other, brother. We can do it again."

"For five years," Isaac said. "Then we realized how stupid that was and started getting together for holidays for our parents' sake. Mom and Dad won't live forever, you know."

"Neither will we. And I won't spend my life consorting with a person who'd sell me out the first chance he got. *Persons*," he corrected, sending Kendall a dark look.

"I'm not selling you out," she defended. "I'm trying to find a way out of this everyone can live with."

"Then you haven't been listening to anything I've said," Max told her. "I'm not doing the show. I'm not living in LA. I'm not lying for my brother—not again. The only way this works—" he gestured between the two of them "—is if you don't pretend to be with him."

"Why?" she finally asked. "Why wouldn't I pretend to be with him?" She ignored the irritation on Max's face and went on. "What reason do I have to stay with you? There's nothing in this town for me. And you refuse to go anywhere. Hell, you've sworn off the whole state of California at this point. Is there something you need to tell me? Some reason for your possessiveness?"

She pleaded with her eyes for him to confess. She knew what she wanted to hear. That, as unlikely as it was, he'd fallen in love with her while she was staying in his cabin. That he couldn't picture living without her. That he would be willing to move heaven and earth for her—when really all he'd have to do was appear on camera saying a few lines his fans were sure to love. It was so little to ask of him, and yet he couldn't seem to do it.

"If you leave with him, you'll never find out." Max held her gaze one more moment before turning and tromping upstairs. She sagged on the chair, eyes unseeing, chest caving in, feeling the weight of those words. Words she hadn't wanted to hear. She'd longed to be comforted. Longed for Max to tell her how he felt. Instead, it was Isaac who comforted her.

"I'm sorry for him." Isaac took the chair next to her and rested his hand over both of hers. "He's being a dick and it's not your fault. It's mine. He's just taking it out on you."

Isaac was probably right, but what good did it do her? She couldn't allow Max to demand she stay here when he'd essentially offered her nothing. He was either blind to what had happened between them, or too damn stubborn to admit it.

She deserved better.

Her brother, Quin, had always told her she deserved a happy, joyous, no-holds-barred life.

Apparently, she was going to have to do what she had to do to get it. No one was going to hand it to her. There were no big breaks, except for the ones you made for yourself. And she'd had a huge one when Max agreed to film the commercial.

She was going to run with it.

Flipping her hand over, she gently squeezed Isaac's hand in hers. He was a good client, a good friend. "If we trust each other, there's no reason why we can't let the public believe whatever they like. You deserve this reunion show. You deserve an abundant career doing what you love."

He smiled, and she could see the gratitude reflected in his eyes, how much this career meant to him. A career Max would gladly endanger in the name of getting his way.

"So do you, Kendall." Isaac gave her fingers another squeeze and then let her go. "I'll do whatever I can to help you rise to the top of the Legacy agency. Someday, you'll own the place if I have anything to say about it."

Grateful, she smiled. Then bitterness crept in. Because as nice as it was to have a friend and client like Isaac, she wished she could have heard those words from Max. From the man she had foolishly fallen in love with.

Twenty-One

Max hadn't believed his own eyes when Kendall and Isaac left at six the next morning to catch a flight.

She hadn't come to bed with him. She hadn't asked him why he'd trotted out an ultimatum, either. He supposed it was just as well. If she'd accused him of caring about her, he'd have had to admit he did care about her. A lot. He couldn't afford to care about anyone that much. Every time in his past he'd allowed himself to "care", it had come back to bite him in the ass.

As for Isaac, Max had shared too much with his brother already. A family. A career. His face, for God's sake. He was *not* sharing Kendall. A moot point. They'd made their choice, and had both walked out on him. It was a choice they'd made together. A choice they'd forced on him.

Max had been forced into plenty of choices over the years when it came to Isaac. Like that damn county fair Isaac had signed him up for. It had been in Arizona, in the blazing July sun. They were supposed to sign headshots, and welcome a washed-up boy band to the stage afterwards. Max hadn't wanted to be the opening act for any band, let alone one performing at a fair. He'd told Isaac as much.

Isaac had ignored Max, and had promoted the event instead. And because Max had a soft spot for his brother, he'd once again conceded. The fair had been as hot as he'd imagined, and they'd signed autographs in the sun for older and younger fans alike. He'd felt like a piece of veal by the end, having to smile and pose for photos, and console crying women who claimed they'd been in love with him since they were twelve years old.

Max had vowed it would be the last time in his life he would let Isaac talk him out of a firm "no." He'd meant it.

That might make Max guilty of holding a grudge in his brother's eyes, but he didn't care what Isaac thought. Kendall wasn't his past, she was his present.

And if she would have refused to play the role of Isaac's girlfriend for packs of rabid paparazzi, she could have been his future.

Two weeks later

Luca called asking if Max wanted to have a beer with him at Vera's, and after a couple of weeks of feeling embittered, alone, angry and sad—all at varying degrees, Max decided to say yes.

The small bar was comfortable and nearly empty when he walked in. Luca was easy to spot, hunkered over the bar, his fist wrapped around a bottle of beer. His goatee was in need of a trim, the bits at his cheeks having filled in with thick, black hair. He shoved his glasses up on his nose when he spotted Max.

"I see you started without me," Max said, shaking the other man's hand.

"I was here early. It's been a hell of a week."

"Tell me about it." Max ordered a beer from the bartender, who coincidentally *was* Vera. "Thanks, V."

"No problem. I've been seeing a lot of you on television. Nice to see you in person." She slung a bar towel over her shoulder and propped one fist on her thick hip. She had short, short gray hair, a healthy waistline and a shrewd stare. Born and raised in Virginia, her accent was tried and true.

"Not me, Vera. *Isaac.*" He took a hearty swallow of beer, tired of trotting out the lie he'd been forced to tell. "Honest mistake."

"I'll be damned." She frowned, as if second-guessing herself, and he realized he was doing the very thing he'd sworn not to… Pretending.

But not for Isaac's sake. For Kendall's.

Even though she'd walked out on him with little more than a handshake goodbye, he cared about her enough to protect her career. He supposed that had a ripple effect. By keeping up with the ruse, he was protecting Isaac's career, as well as keeping himself out of the spotlight. Win/win/win, he thought miserably.

Vera wandered to the other side of the bar to greet a couple taking their seats, and that's when Luca called Max on his bullshit.

"I've seen the commercial. The girl is as pretty as you said."

"I never said."

"You didn't have to." His friend chuckled. "Isaac might look like you, but you hold yourself differently than he does. I'd have to be blind to think it was anyone but you in that commercial, Max."

"Didn't know you were a *Brooks Knows Best* superfan." Max was willing to fudge the truth to the locals, but he refused to lie to Luca. The man had been in his life since Max moved to Dunn…before it was renamed Dunn. "I can autograph something for you if you like."

"You have everyone snowed, man, but you forget." His friend spread his arms and grinned. "Snow's my business. I recognize it when I see it. Why lie to sweet Vera?"

Max sent a furtive glance to "sweet" Vera, who was telling a filthy joke to the busboy. He shook his head. "I don't want recognition for the commercial."

"Or," Luca amended, "you're hiding out with a broken heart."

"I thought you said you knew me. What are the chances of me having a broken heart?" Max laughed aloud at the notion. A broken heart was something a

fourteen-year-old version of himself might have suffered, not the adult version.

"Bunny hurt you." Luca clearly wasn't pulling
any punches today. "We all saw it. How you holed
up afterward. You were determined to make a life
out of being by yourself."

"Remind me not to accept further invitations for
beers from you."

Unfazed, his pal continued. "You were resolute
about the split with Bunny. When you two split, you
handled it like a business transaction. Now Kendall
is dating your brother, and you look…" Luca exam-
ined Max carefully. "You look like dog shit."

Max drained his beer and signaled Vera for a refill. Evidently, he was going to need it. She made
quick work of the refill and asked if they wanted to
order dinner.

"Yeah." Max shot a thumb at Luca. "He's buying."

They both ordered club sandwiches, which was,
hands down, the best dish at Vera's.

"She's not dating Isaac," Max clarified. "You're
snowed after all if you believe what you read online."

"How do you know? Have you talked to her?"

"You think I'm so easily replaced by my brother?"
He tried to be assertive, but he didn't sound as resolute as he would have liked. As much as he'd cared for
Kendall, he had let her go to California without him.
And without telling her how he felt, because face it,
he hadn't been able to put his feelings into words with
his brother present, clouding his judgment.

Like when he'd sent her off to her hotel in the blizzard and she'd suffered the accident, Max blamed himself for her leaving with his brother. And now, she was pretending to be Isaac's girlfriend. It was insanity. He'd tried to avoid searching online for their photos, but his curiosity had won the best of him on a random sleepless night.

The paps had snapped photos of Isaac and Kendall laughing together at a coffee shop. They'd also snapped photos of them holding hands—which Max really didn't like. And one photo, his least favorite, had featured his brother whispering into her ear. Isaac could be charming, no doubt about it. But Max wasn't worried about Kendall falling for Isaac's charms. He was worried about *Isaac* falling for her. As Max knew from experience, she was damn easy to fall for, and he hadn't been trying. If Isaac felt one-tenth of what Max felt for her, his brother would fight to keep her at his side.

Which was a great bit more than Max had done in a similar circumstance.

"I don't know what to think." Luca regarded Max with bemusement. "You don't typically roll over and show your belly. But you look positively whipped now that you let her leave."

"How do you know I let her leave?"

"Because she left. Woman like that comes into your life, one who makes you tromp out in the snow and kick your own ass for her bonking her car into a tree, you don't let her leave. You drop to your knees and beg her to stay."

"And if she refuses to stay? Then what?"

"You asked her to stay?"

"Not exactly. It was implied."

Luca shook his head like he was disappointed. That made two of them.

"If the woman you love leaves, then you follow her wherever she goes until you can talk her into coming back to you."

"You don't understand. You were raised in North Dakota."

"Portugal and then North Dakota," Luca reminded him.

"Portugal *and then* North Dakota," Max repeated. He'd known Luca had been born in Portugal, but he'd lived there only until he was three years old. "Point being, you weren't raised in Hollywood. You don't know what that town is like. What it can do to a person."

"Well, if you're any example, I'd say it can rob you of your good sense."

Max sent his buddy a warning glare that went ignored.

"Followed a woman to Chicago once," Luca confessed. "Didn't work out."

"You've never mentioned Chicago."

"It was a long time ago. And not fun to talk about."

Max understood. He didn't want to talk about Kendall, either.

"I never gathered the courage to tell her how I felt. Ended up leaving instead, looking for something else. I thought what I needed was a change of scenery."

That sounded familiar, so Max didn't comment.

"Dunn was gaining in popularity as a *little big town*, and as you said, I'm a *Brooks Knows Best* superfan. I wanted to be close to you." He clapped Max on the shoulder and let out a hearty laugh. Max rolled his eyes at his friend's sarcasm. "Also, my cousin Rafael lives here and wouldn't shut up about it. One visit, I was hooked. It's a great town."

"The best," Max agreed. "If Kendall would have shared your feelings, we wouldn't be here discussing her choosing California and my brother."

"Some of us follow our hearts, not our brains."

"Don't you mean your balls, not your brains?"

"I mean my heart." Luca tapped his chest.

"What about now? Still following your heart?"

"Yes. I just haven't met the right woman. Unlike you."

"There is no right woman. If I've learned anything from my failed marriage, it's that it taught me to be more careful with my proclamations about the future."

"Coward," Luca said as Vera set their sandwiches in front of them. "Trust me. I know from experience."

"It's wisdom, Luca," Max said after Vera had left them to eat. "I learn from my mistakes."

They each downed half of their sandwiches before Luca spoke again. "If you can't look forward and have hope, there's really nowhere else to look."

"You can look back. And learn lessons from the past."

"Yes. You can also let that past force you into hiding in a mountain town pretending to be no one."

"My dream come true." Max forced a grin as he chewed a French fry.

"Max the loner. It must be nice not needing people," Luca said thoughtfully, his eyes on the television. It just so happened the Citizen watch commercial came on next. Vera sent a curious glance to the TV and then to Max, like she was doubting his denial.

Max watched his on-screen self take Kendall into his arms. His chest hollowed out as the memories of her in his bed rained down over him. The thought of Isaac taking her into his arms—or worse, into his bed—made Max want to howl.

"Max the loner," Luca repeated. "Sure you don't want to book a flight to California after all?"

Silently, Max turned from the television, feeling emptier than when he'd arrived. "I promised I'd never see her again if she walked out. It's a promise I intend to keep."

He'd let her in to his life, his world, and like his ex, Kendall had changed. She'd gone from having eyes only for him to running off with the more profitable Dunn brother.

He'd been right about Kendall Squire the first time he'd laid eyes on her. She was Hollywood through and through.

He'd keep his promise not to speak to her again if it killed him, and the way things were going right about now, it damn well might.

Twenty-Two

"Swing me around and let me see! Just a quick peek," Meghan begged on the video call.

"Fine, but then I have to hang up on you. The interview is about to start." Kendall tapped her phone's screen so that the camera faced the studio. Isaac was sitting on the sofa, an assistant attaching a microphone to his lapel while the host recapped what they'd be discussing. "There. Are you happy?" Kendall whispered when Meghan was facing her again.

"Happy that you are on the set of my favorite talk show with my favorite actor of all time without me?" Meghan frowned. "No. I'm not happy."

Kendall gave her sister a wan smile. "I promised you'll meet him."

She expected her sister to give her crap for not

fulfilling that promise, and maybe trot out another oh-so-jealous mini rant. Instead, Meg's returning smile was pitying.

"I love you. You're going to be fine." Her sister knew everything. About the commercial, about Max and Isaac's argument, about Kendall being in love with Max and Max trotting out an ultimatum. About how Kendall was pretending to be Isaac's love interest for the sake of both of their careers.

She'd called her sister last week, using her laptop so she could be hands free. She needed her hands for pouring a glass of wine and wiping away her tears while she explained how Max Dunn was a selfish jackass.

Since then, Meg had called daily to check in on her. Kendall wasn't as fragile as she had been that night, but she certainly wasn't any less heartbroken. As she'd told her sister yesterday evening, Kendall was hurt that Max didn't care about her as much as she cared about him. "He should have respected me and my career enough to let me make those decisions for myself," she'd told her sister. "Without the threat of losing him."

Meghan had agreed, and worse, Isaac had agreed. Kendall had been tempted to give Max the benefit of the doubt, but facts were facts. She was back in Los Angeles, playing her part for the sake of the best ad dollars she'd seen in her career, and for Isaac's reputation in connection with *Brooks Knows Best*.

Which meant she had recently come to a new conclusion about herself. One that didn't give her the benefit of the doubt, either. In a quiet corner and out of sight from the cameramen, Kendall admitted to her sister, "I chose my career over Max."

"No. No, honey. You have bills to pay and goals to reach."

"He warned me against pursuing success." He'd been right. Here she was, "successful" and feeling absolutely awful about it. "I'd rather have love than money."

"I'd rather have both," Meghan said. "Sadly, money has never been my strong suit. And you know, my love life isn't looking so hot, either. What gives?"

Kendall laughed at her sister's earnest delivery. Meghan was funny, adorable and, admittedly, bad with money.

"I believe you can have love and success, Kendall. Just because *he* didn't want to exit his comfort zone for you doesn't mean you're not lovable. It means his head is currently located in his ass."

"I screwed up. Pretending…" She paused to look around to double-check she wasn't being overheard. "*Being* with Isaac isn't the same." Because she liked him just fine, but she didn't love him. They'd done the bare minimum for the paparazzi, which hadn't amounted to more than holding hands, but it still felt wrong.

"It's only for a little while longer. And when you call it quits, you can have an exclusive interview on my podcast to do damage control. I insist."

"I'm in love with him." In the screen-in-screen of her phone, she watched her own chin wobble.

"I know you are, honey." Megan knew exactly who Kendall was referring to. "I wish he was worthy of you."

The cameraman began counting down as the studio lights went up. Kendall waved goodbye to her sister and ended the call, silencing her phone so as not to disturb the taping.

Thankfully her professional mode snapped into place the second she walked to the edge of the stage to watch the taping. She'd been wrong about her acting skills. She was better at it than she thought. She had convinced the world she was falling for Isaac, hiding the fact that she'd been falling apart every day for the last two weeks. Someone should give her an award.

On the inside she was a wreck. She'd taken to working from home lately to avoid the drive to the office. The walk from the parking lot was worse now that there were photographers lurking in the bushes.

She'd begun to understand why Max felt the way he did about this town. She'd never been on the other side of the camera lens before she shot the commercial with Max. At the time she'd been so sure no one would notice her. If she'd have known the outcome, she might never have filmed it.

A lie, she thought with a sad smile. She'd have done it if only to share those moments with Max. Unfortunately, those moments were preserved for everyone to watch and rewatch—including her.

The talk show, *What Wendi Watts*, was hosted by comedienne Wendi Watts. She belted out her signature laugh, almost as loud as her bright orange dress. The show was a hit with fans of every age and gender. It was a huge spot to land for Isaac.

Objectively, Kendall could be happy for him. Personally, she wished she'd have skipped today's taping. She'd accompanied Isaac for practical reasons. They were scheduled to visit the producer of *Brooks Knows Best* and discuss shooting schedule changes. It was Kendall's job to make sure the show wasn't bending the contract—a favorite pastime of some producers. But being here while Wendi prodded Isaac about his love life was brutal. Especially when the sexy commercial of Kendall and Max began playing on the screen behind Isaac.

"Look at you two!" Wendi playfully slapped Isaac's knee. "You practically had sex in this commercial. I love it."

Isaac, with a practiced made-for-TV smile, kept his composure. "Kendall is an amazing woman. Inside and out. It's cool that the ad spot resonated so well with fans. We really didn't expect this much attention."

"She's here today, isn't she?" Wendi made a show of looking past the camera lenses. "I see you, girl! Get your pretty face out here and say hi."

Kendall shook her head vehemently. She was dressed up and had applied her makeup for their meeting later, but she was in no way camera-ready.

"Come on, sweetheart." Isaac stood and offered a hand. Before she knew it, she was being hauled under the bright lights and plunking down on the couch facing Wendi Watts.

"I mean, look at this." Wendi signaled for the video to resume playing.

Kendall watched, her stomach in knots. Lying about dating Isaac hadn't required her to verbally lie until just now. Wendi paused the video again and blinked at Kendall, expectant.

"She's not used to the attention yet." Isaac wove his fingers with Kendall's to cover for her silence.

"Is he worth it?" Wendi cocked her head. "If asked, I'd say the man in this commercial was totally worth the trouble."

"He was. Is," she hastily corrected with a nervous smile.

Wendi turned her attention to Isaac, asking how he'd prepared for his returning role in *Brooks Knows Best*. As Isaac gave a scripted answer, Kendall let his voice fade into the background.

After this interview, he would have to attend future events without her. She would be there for contract dealings, like the one with the studio this afternoon, but these sorts of acts would have to stop. She couldn't live with herself if she had to lie about them any longer.

Even if he fired her, she refused to pretend to be in love with him—or appear to be in love with him—for another minute. Her brother's dying wish was for her to achieve success in this town, but he'd also been twenty years old when he died. He had no idea how many twists and turns she'd have to handle. A career she loved meant something to her, but it didn't mean everything. She would trade her newfound success to have Quin back. To have Max back.

The former was an impossibility, but there might still be hope for the latter. She stood from the couch, dropping Isaac's hand in the process. He frowned up at her while Wendi joked about Kendall having a more pressing matter than "her man's interview."

Kendall opened her mouth to apologize, at the same time a deep, resonant voice boomed in the air.

"Wrong man."

She turned her head to find Max Dunn stepping onto the set in all his flannel-and-blue-jeans-wearing glory, his mouth a displeased line and his eyebrows set low over his nose.

"It appears we have a surprise guest," Wendi chirped without missing a beat. "Max Dunn! Isaac's missing-in-action twin brother." A set dresser rushed in with an additional chair for Max—as if he was in any condition to sit down. He looked as if he might tear the set apart wall by wall, and smash Wendi's branded coffee mugs into the rubble afterward.

"Have a seat, Max," Wendi encouraged, either not picking up on or ignoring his body language. He was positively vibrating with anger. Kendall lowered onto the couch, unable to stand now that the man she loved had voluntarily burst onto a stage in front of live cameras.

"Max?" Wendi prompted.

Ignoring the talk show's host completely, he lowered to a squatting position in front of Kendall and placed his hands on either side of her body. Her own hands trembled. She had to clasp them together to keep from reaching for him. He was here. Really here. But, why?

"Those photos of the two of you together," Max started, his voice low and only for her. He licked his lower lip and started again. "Are the photos of you and Isaac online the real deal, or are you still faking it?"

"Max," she whispered, scared to believe he was here for the reason she hoped he was: to admit he made a colossal mistake in letting her go.

"I'll do the walk-on for *Brooks Knows Best*," he continued. "I'll sign autographs at a county fair. I'll film another Citizen commercial. Hell, I'll make commercials for laundry detergent if I have to. As long as you swear you'll stop letting everyone believe you're in love with my brother. You're not, are you?"

His eyebrows bent like he was actually worried. As if she could turn around and fall for Isaac as easily as she'd fallen for Max.

She palmed his cheek. "Poor, stupid man."

He frowned, appeared confused. God love him.

"Wait, if I'm getting this right," Wendi interrupted, frantically waving her hands in front of her face, "*Max* is the Dunn brother in the commercial? Not Isaac?"

"Max, the favorite Dunn brother," Isaac confirmed, "was the one who filmed the commercial. I can't grow a beard that thick."

"He can't." Max flicked a glance to his brother.

"He has a scar on his chin from me pushing him off a stage one time. If he grows a full beard, he has a huge slash through it."

"I deserved it," Isaac told Wendi with a smile.

"You didn't," Max argued.

Isaac's smile vanished, and he gave his brother a slow, understanding nod.

It wasn't a full reconciliation, but Kendall thought it could be the start of an understanding between them.

"So, Max, if anyone was questioning your acting skills before, they now know you're as good as you ever were," Wendi said, attempting to salvage her interview.

"I'm not as good as Isaac," Max said, "but to answer your question, Wendi, I wasn't acting. I was falling in love in real time." He took both of Kendall's hands and stood with her. "I don't pretend with you, California. I never did."

The studio fell away as she wrapped her arms around his neck and kissed him, vaguely aware of Isaac's chuckle and Wendi's gasp of surprise.

"Did you just do what I thought you did?" she asked as he hugged her close.

"Admit I'm in love with you on national television?" He turned his head to take in the cameras' unblinking black eyes. Then he sent a look to his brother, who grinned anew. "Yeah, I think I did."

"In that case," she said, "allow me to return the

sentiment." She fisted his shirt and dragged his face to hers. Nose to nose with him, she said, "I love you, too, Max Dunn."

Epilogue

A week later...

"White or red?" Kendall held up two bottles of wine for Max to choose from. He was leaning against her tidy kitchen counter in her apartment, appearing indecisive. Also appearing hotter than hell given the backdrop of palm trees and blue skies behind him. "How is it that you don't like it here when you look so good in this setting?"

His smile was slow but persistent. Soon he was grinning and walking her way before wrapping a hand around her hip and tugging her close. He took the wine bottles from her hands and set them on the counter, leaned in and lit her on fire with one of his signature Max Dunn kisses.

When he was finished, he pulled back and smiled at his handiwork: namely, her, bracing the counter-top to keep from sliding down the side of it and into a puddle on the floor. She cleared her head, and then her throat, and tried again.

"White or red?"

"Either one is fine with me, California. Isaac's the picky one."

"I heard that," came a voice through the screen door at the front of her apartment. Isaac let him-self in, carrying—how about that—a bottle of white wine.

"White it is." Kendall accepted the bottle when he offered it to her. "Oh, and it's chilled. Well done, you." She moved to the cabinet to pull down glass-ware, listening as Max and Isaac chatted casually about life in general. From behind a cabinet door, she hid a smile.

The Wendi Watts show had gone on after Ken-dall and Max had declared their love for each other. When they ducked behind the cameras once again, Isaac had stayed to explain the situation to Wendi. He'd smoothed over the pretend relationship between him and Kendall by explaining how she'd been help-ing him cover for the real love of his life. A woman he'd taken to his private island, though Isaac refused to share why.

The story was a crock, but Wendi bought it. The eager talk show host promptly forgot the former bombshell of Max and Isaac's twin switch and moved on to the juicier one: Isaac's secret love life.

Isaac had continued with the farce, proclaiming, "I promised her I wouldn't say anything until she's ready."

Hence, this small gathering at Kendall's apartment with wine. And pizza, whenever the delivery arrived. She shut the cabinet door and tuned in to the discussion currently happening between the Dunn brothers.

"...unless you want to do the commercial instead of me?" Isaac asked Max with a grin.

Max glared.

"Our decision is final." She handed Isaac and Max each a wineglass before palming her own. "Max and I have had enough media attention for a lifetime. Should we sit on the balcony?"

Her apartment's balcony was small but the view was great. Well, great for what she paid for this place. They went outside to her rattan furniture and enjoyed the perfect seventy-something weather.

"Have you found the love of your life yet to show off to the public?" she teased.

"I wondered how long it'd take you to bring that up." Isaac smirked. Clean-shaven now, he looked a little less like Max, who still sported a full beard. Isaac's smirk vanished a second later. "One of the reasons I wanted to come out tonight, besides to visit my brother before he goes back home to Virginia forever, was to surrender."

"Surrender what?" Max lazed back in his chair, his hand encircling the top of his wineglass.

Isaac's expression was almost abashed. "I can't find anyone who would willingly step into the crosshairs with me." He took a hearty gulp of his wine, filling his cheeks before pointing at Kendall. "You're going to find her for me."

Max's crack of laughter was lost on the soft breeze. "She's your agent, not a magician."

"Well, she *did* land Bunny a role on *Brooks Knows Best*," Isaac pointed out. "That was pretty fucking magical."

Max tilted his head in consideration before acquiescing. "Good point." Then he, too, looked at Kendall. "Know any single girls?"

"In Los Angeles? A ton. But most are clients of the agency and have their own careers to think about."

"How about Dunn?" Isaac looked to Max. "Now that the show has moved the shoot to your town instead of LA, are there any single ladies who would play pretend with me for a few months?"

"Helen's very kind," Kendall said of the elderly coffee shop owner.

Isaac gave her a bland blink. "I know Helen. You're very funny."

"Is it a good idea to trot out another fake relationship?" Max asked his brother, reaching for Kendall's hand in silent claim as he did.

Isaac didn't miss the possessive move, but his eyes

quickly rerouted from hers and Max's linked hands to the mountains behind them. He squinted against the sunshine. "Is it a good idea to admit I was lying to cover up for the first lie?"

Another good point. Right now the public adored Isaac and had been excited to hear he had a secret love. If he admitted he'd made it up, it could hurt his reputation, and in turn, the reputation of the show he'd worked so hard on.

"It wouldn't hurt to be in the public eye with someone, even if the relationship fizzled out later," she considered.

"You've got to be kidding." Max shook his head.

"It'll be great promo for the show. The fans like to see Isaac happy."

"I am happy," Isaac argued, but she wasn't so sure. He'd absconded to a private island to be completely alone to prepare for a show he was terrified he'd screw up. "I'm more concerned about being irrelevant. Again."

He swallowed that admission with the remainder of his wine when the doorbell rang. "Pizza guy. I'll get it." He disappeared into her apartment.

She immediately turned to Max. "A fake girlfriend for him isn't a half-bad idea."

"It's the worst idea I've ever heard. What if the girl who agrees to be his fake girlfriend has a man on the other side of the country who's completely in love with her?" He kissed Kendall's hand. "And then he calls every connection he has in LA to track her down, learns she's on the Wendi Watts show, and barges into the studio mid-interview to proclaim his love for her in front of the world?"

Kendall grinned, unable to keep from it. Thinking of the way he showed up for her—putting her first and his distaste for fame in the rearview— made her fall in love with him a little more. "I doubt that scenario would replay itself over again. That seems like the kind of thing that happens once in a lifetime."

"The TV studio thing, or falling in love when he swore not to thing?"

"I don't know. Both?"

"Yeah, both." He set his wineglass and hers aside and physically pulled her onto his lap. "The falling-in-love part is guaranteed to only happen once in my lifetime." He paused, looking around at her view. "Will you miss it here?"

She sighed as she took in the smoggy scenery interspersed with palm trees and mountains. The crowded buildings and concrete walkways, the corner store she visited every other day because she didn't have enough cabinet space to stock up, and her apartment, nestled in the middle of all of it.

She shook her head. "I think I've done what I need to do here. I'm looking forward to seeing what the next part of my life brings."

"You'll figure out how to be a talent agent from afar. Airplanes fly into LA from Virginia."

"Unless there's a major blizzard."

He moved her hair behind her ear and kissed her. "Unless."

"Love you, Mountain Man."

"Love you, too, California."

She kissed him again, snuggling close as he held her tight. The breeze blew, and it was as if her brother's approval weaved through the strands of her hair.

She could almost hear his raspy voice on the wind. A nearly indistinguishable "Nice goin', sis," she heard with her heart.

* * * * *

Look for Isaac's story,
coming in spring 2022!

SPECIAL EXCERPT FROM

⬧ HARLEQUIN
DESIRE

*Alaskan senator Jessup Outlaw needs an escape…
and he finds just what he needs on his Napa Valley
vacation: actress Paige Novak. What starts as a fling
soon gets serious, but a familiar face from Paige's past
may ruin everything…*

Read on for a sneak peek of
What Happens on Vacation…
by New York Times *bestselling author Brenda Jackson.*

"Hey, aren't you going to join me?" Paige asked, pushing wet hair back from her face and treading water in the center of the pool. "Swimming is on my list of fun things. We might as well kick things off with a bang."

Bang? Why had she said that? Lust immediately took over his senses. Desire beyond madness consumed him. He was determined that by the time they parted ways at the end of the month their sexual needs, wants and desires would be fulfilled and under control.

Quickly removing his shirt, Jess's hands went to his zipper, inched it down and slid the pants, along with his briefs, down his legs. He knew Paige was watching him and he was glad that he was the man she wanted.

"Come here, Paige."

She smiled and shook her head. "If you want me, Jess, you have to come and get me." She then swam to the far end of the pool, away from him.

Oh, so now she wanted to play hard to get? He had no problem going after her. Maybe now was a good time to tell her that not only had he been captain of his dog sled team, but he'd also been captain of his college swim team.

He glided through the water like an Olympic swimmer going after the gold, and it didn't take long to reach her. When she saw him getting close, she laughed and swam to the other side. Without missing a stroke or losing speed, he did a freestyle flip turn and reached out and caught her by the ankles. The capture was swift and the minute he touched her, more desire rammed through him to the point where water couldn't cool him down.

"I got you," he said, pulling her toward him and swimming with her in his arms to the edge of the pool.

When they reached the shallow end, he allowed her to stand, and the minute her feet touched the bottom she circled her arms around his neck. "No, Jess, I got you and I'm ready for you." Then she leaned in and took his mouth.

Don't miss what happens next in...
What Happens on Vacation...
by Brenda Jackson, the next book in her
Westmoreland Legacy: The Outlaws series!

Available March 2022 wherever
Harlequin Desire books and ebooks are sold.

Harlequin.com

Get 4 FREE REWARDS!

We'll send you 2 FREE Books plus 2 FREE Mystery Gifts.

Harlequin Desire books transport you to the world of the American elite with juicy plot twists, delicious sensuality and intriguing scandal.

FREE Value Over $20

YES! Please send me 2 FREE Harlequin Desire novels and my 2 FREE gifts (gifts are worth about $10 retail). After receiving them, if I don't wish to receive any more books, I can return the shipping statement marked "cancel." If I don't cancel, I will receive 6 brand-new novels every month and be billed just $4.55 per book in the U.S. or $5.24 per book in Canada. That's a savings of at least 13% off the cover price! It's quite a bargain! Shipping and handling is just 50¢ per book in the U.S. and $1.25 per book in Canada.* I understand that accepting the 2 free books and gifts places me under no obligation to buy anything. I can always return a shipment and cancel at any time. The free books and gifts are mine to keep no matter what I decide.

225/326 HDN GNND

Name (please print)

Address   Apt. #

City   State/Province   Zip/Postal Code

Email: Please check this box ☐ if you would like to receive newsletters and promotional emails from Harlequin Enterprises ULC and its affiliates. You can unsubscribe anytime.

Mail to the Harlequin Reader Service:
IN U.S.A.: P.O. Box 1341, Buffalo, NY 14240-8531
IN CANADA: P.O. Box 603, Fort Erie, Ontario L2A 5X3

Want to try 2 free books from another series! Call 1-800-873-8635 or visit www.ReaderService.com.

*Terms and prices subject to change without notice. Prices do not include sales taxes, which will be charged (if applicable) based on your state or country of residence. Canadian residents will be charged applicable taxes. Offer not valid in Quebec. This offer is limited to one order per household. Books received may not be as shown. Not valid for current subscribers to Harlequin Desire books. All orders subject to approval. Credit or debit balances in a customer's account(s) may be offset by any other outstanding balance owed by or to the customer. Please allow 4 to 6 weeks for delivery. Offer available while quantities last.

Your Privacy—Your information is being collected by Harlequin Enterprises ULC, operating as Harlequin Reader Service. For a complete summary of the information we collect, how we use this information and to whom it is disclosed, please visit our privacy notice located at corporate.harlequin.com/privacy-notice. From time to time we may also exchange your personal information with reputable third parties. If you wish to opt out of this sharing of your personal information, please visit readerservice.com/consumerschoice or call 1-800-873-8635. **Notice to California Residents**—Under California law, you have specific rights to control and access your data. For more information on these rights and how to exercise them, visit corporate.harlequin.com/california-privacy.

HD21R2

HARLEQUIN

Heartfelt or thrilling, passionate or uplifting—Harlequin is more than just happily-ever-after.

With twelve different series to choose from and new books available every month, you are sure to find stories that will move you, uplift you, inspire and delight you.

HNEWS2021

Love Harlequin romance?

DISCOVER.

Be the first to find out about promotions,
news and exclusive content!

 Facebook.com/HarlequinBooks

 Twitter.com/HarlequinBooks

 Instagram.com/HarlequinBooks

 Pinterest.com/HarlequinBooks

 YouTube.com/HarlequinBooks

ReaderService.com

EXPLORE.

Sign up for the Harlequin e-newsletter and
download a free book from any series at
TryHarlequin.com

CONNECT.

Join our Harlequin community to
share your thoughts and connect
with other romance readers!
Facebook.com/groups/HarlequinConnection